Murder at Sea of Passenger X
Georgie Shaw Cozy Mystery #5

Anna Celeste Burke

DEDICATION

To smooth sailing and great adventures
with people we love!

Books by Anna Celeste Burke

Murder at Catmmando Mountain, Georgie Shaw Cozy Mystery #1

Love Notes in the Key of Sea, Georgie Shaw Cozy Mystery #2

All Hallows' Eve Heist, Georgie Shaw Cozy Mystery #3

A Merry Christmas Wedding Mystery, Georgie Shaw Cozy Mystery #4

Murder at Sea of Passenger X, Georgie Shaw Cozy Mystery #5

FIND BOOKS IN THE SERIES HERE:
http://bit.ly/shawcozy

~~~~~

Cowabunga Christmas! Corsario Cove Cozy Mystery #1

Gnarly New Year! Corsario Cove Cozy Mystery #2

Heinous Habits! Corsario Cove Cozy Mystery #3 Out 2017

FIND BOOKS IN THE SERIES HERE:
http://bit.ly/covecozy

~~~~~

A Dead Husband Jessica Huntington Desert Cities Mystery #1

A Dead Sister Jessica Huntington Desert Cities Mystery #2

A Dead Daughter Jessica Huntington Desert Cities Mystery #3

A Dead Mother Jessica Huntington Desert Cities Mystery #4, Out 2017

FIND BOOKS IN THE SERIES HERE:
http://amzn.to/1WMdJrS

Love A Foot Above the Ground Prequel to the Jessica Huntington Desert Cities Mystery Series @ http://smarturl.it/loveabove

CONTENTS

ACKNOWLEDGMENTS

Thanks to my *many-years-husband* who read the first draft of this book and gave me tips on what to fix before it went out to beta readers. That included checking up on some of the technical details about how long it takes to fly to Tahiti in a private jet, security measures taken by cruise lines to keep us safe, and the background required for a chef to get a Michelin star rating. He also recalled some great moments from our cruise through the Society Islands. That trip we took eons ago long before I ever dreamed of writing a story about the place. It was still a great source of inspiration.

Thanks, as well, to Ying Cooper for tackling the proofreading job with skill and grace, as usual.

I'm also grateful for the ongoing support and feedback from readers of Advance Review Copies: Denise Austin, Peggy Hyndman, Doward Wilson, Valerie Bargewell, Andrea Stoeckel, Andra Weis, Jeanine Carlson, Bonnie Dale Keck, Michele Hayes, Jeanie Whitmore Jackson, Karen Vaughan, Donna Wolz, Tara Brown, and Michele Bodenheimer.

1 THE PURRLOINED NOTE

The screams didn't wake me. I was already up by then. I'm not sure what had stirred me from my sleep. Maybe I sensed the sparkling blue eyes gazing intently at me. Two sets since Miles and Ella sat side-by-side in Sphinx mode. Their chocolate ears pointed straight up—radar on!

"What has put you two on high alert?" I had asked my super-sensitive pair of Siamese cats. Talking to my cats was an old habit, usually rewarded by a bellow in return. Not this morning. It was quiet in our lovely suite on an upper deck of the MMW Fantasy of the Sea, one of the newest ships in my megalomaniacal boss's cruise line. That grandiose streak in him isn't all bad. Max Marley had paid for our honeymoon cruise to the South Sea Islands, and arranged for our cats to go along on the adventure, as a wedding present. I'm not ungrateful, just realistic about the gentleman genius who runs Marvelous Marley World, the entertainment conglomerate where I work.

The drapes in our suite were still drawn, but the sliders to the balcony were partly open. A sea breeze blew in, and the fabric billowed. *Jack must have opened it*, I thought, stretching, lazily, as I sank back into the comfy bed.

We both loved the salty air as we ventured from island to island during our ten days at sea. The siren song of adventure was carried along on those breezes for my handsome new husband who spent his life fighting crime as a police detective. For me, they are a reminder of home in Orange County where the Pacific Ocean is a walk away. That's where Jack would live, too, when we returned to California.

As I had discovered during our week of cruising, Jack is an early riser. I enjoy my mornings, too, but I prefer to start my day slowly if I can get away with it. Perhaps that's because I have a harder time than he does falling asleep at night. My anxious spirit wrestles with worries of the day. Jack nods off at the drop of a hat, a defensive strategy he picked up to survive decades as a cop.

"Grab your forty winks when you can," he said. "Crime may not pay, but it doesn't sleep either. You never know when you'll get a call in the middle of the night or at the crack of dawn." That admonition was right up there with another of his favorite guidelines: "eat dessert first."

After dating the man for almost a year before we married, I knew what he meant. We'd had dinner and other plans canceled or interrupted by murder and mischief more than once. My job was no picnic, either. Marvelous Marley World isn't always marvelous as Jack has pointed out on more than one occasion. Several of those rescheduled dates had resulted from hijinks in the Arcadia theme park or elsewhere at Marvelous Marley World.

I yawned. It was tempting to doze off again, but a missive of my own changed my mind. A line by the ancient poet Rumi. *The breeze at dawn has secrets to tell you. Don't go back to sleep.* Grabbing the lovely silk robe a new friend had given me at my bridal shower, I slipped it on, along with a pair of slippers.

When I pulled back the curtains, I hoped Jack would be lounging on the balcony that ran the length of our suite. Not there.

"Where's your daddy?" I asked the feline duo still sitting on my bed. Their ears moved at odd angles, in every direction. I laughed at the silly motions. "If you guys are trying to send me signals, it's not working!"

"Jack," I called out as I moved from the bedroom to the adjoining living room and dining area. No luck. The drapes were already pulled back in this room, and the sun poured in. All the polished wood, brass trim, and stone surfaces sparkled. I paused for a moment, as the dazzling blue waters took my breath away. Off in the distance, I could see a craggy peak rising from the sea. Bora Bora was our last stop before heading back to Tahiti, for a flight to Maui. I took a deep breath relishing the idea that another ten days of island life awaited us before returning to the hustle and bustle of our careers.

Where could he be? I wondered, feeling just a tinge of concern. It wasn't like Jack to step out without telling me first or leaving a note. He hadn't been in our master bath. Maybe Jack was in the bathroom off the second bedroom in our sprawling penthouse suite that was way too large for the two of us. Even "Mad" Max Marley's generosity was over the top at times, as was the inspiration he drew from the sea for this fantasy ship.

A video mural graced the walls in this room featuring interactive screens that displayed a realistic underwater world that sprang to life as I moved toward the second master suite. Max's wild imaginings were everywhere on this cruise ship in what I can only describe as a Walt Disney meets Dr. Seuss experience. Max never skimped, though, and the entire cruise line was top-rate.

It would be just like my kind husband to shower in the secondary bathroom so the noise wouldn't wake me. I guessed correctly. Damp towels were hanging over the side of the hamper to dry. Jack had been there, but he was gone now!

I suddenly felt alone. A crazy thought popped into my head: *Had I lost him like the first man to whom I had become engaged?* Danny had simply disappeared one evening long ago, after a vicious attack on the beach. The haunting strains of *Love Notes in the Key of Sea*, the song my fiancé had written for me before he went missing, meandered through my mind. An eerie reminder that life isn't always about happy endings.

"Oh, stop it, Georgina Shaw!" I chastised myself aloud. "We're on a cruise ship, for goodness' sake, out in the calm, open sea still a good distance from land. Where could he go? If he's not back in an hour, I'll call the Captain and tell him my husband has gone missing." The cats had joined me. Miles, the older of the two, boomed in a voice that had earned him his name. My fine, feline's caterwauling is as distinctive as the trumpet played by my favorite jazz master, Miles Davis.

"Don't worry, Miles, I'm talking to myself, not you." It did not elude me that the statement made it possible to remove "cat" from "crazy cat lady." I had long ago accepted the term reserved for women who regularly hold conversations with their feline companions. Miles peered at me, as though trying so hard to understand what I was saying that I laughed. He yowled again, and Ella mimicked him in tones that were more melodious. She was a smaller, younger version of Miles—a gift from Jack that had made our little family complete.

Both my cats, like many of their species I suspect, have an uncanny ability to pick up the emotions around them. Most likely, Miles was reflecting my anxious feelings. Not that he can read my mind or anything quite like that. Cats notice the smallest changes in their territory and I assume that includes the people around them. I had been wary about bringing the cats along on our honeymoon—another part of Mad Max's master plan. Fortunately, after a day spent inspecting every inch of the suite and patrolling the premises, Miles and Ella settled in and made themselves at home.

Suddenly, Miles raised his head, pointed his nose to the sky, and bellowed. Some show I watched once said that house cats don't roar. Wrong! This utterance was no meow. As was often the case, that roar was an alert sent out seconds before Jack's arrival. I attribute it to Miles' keen sense of hearing, but who knows?

The door handle wiggled, and then the door sprang open. There, in all his glory, stood my missing husband. A Panama hat sat jauntily on his head above a pair of dark glasses that gave him the air of a movie star. Hollywood or not, he was my leading man, and I felt a familiar snap, crackle, pop sensation ripple through me.

"Hello, Doll," he said in a mock detective voice. The love we shared for old film noir detective movies was almost as great as the enjoyment we got from Jazz classics.

"I see you're wearing the anniversary gifts I set out for you last night. Where have you been? Not out detecting, I hope, while your new wife wakes up to an empty suite." I wanted to scold him, but the smile on his handsome face melted my resolve.

He was loaded down with packages. I caught a hint of fresh-baked pastry. Coffee, too. From one arm hung a lei of fresh orchids. I rushed to help him unload those packages. By the time, I reached him he had managed to set them down on a bar near the door. Those empty arms were around me in an instant.

"The only mystery I'm interested in solving is the mystery of what makes you so gorgeous even before you comb your hair or put on any makeup." The kiss that went with that bit of blarney rattled me to my toes.

Once he released me from that embrace, I tugged the front of his hat down. He took that hat off and sailed it across the room to a chair in the corner. Two cats flew after it, jumping up in that chair to inspect it. Then Jack took off the shades and tucked them into a pocket of his colorful aloha shirt.

"Didn't you find my poetic love note?" He asked as he placed that garland of flowers around my neck. "For my bride of one whole week."

"Fresh cut flowers on a cruise ship at sea. Mad Max Marley does have a knack for making dreams come true, doesn't he?"

"The man is a class act—when he's not in mad-hatter mode."

"Where did you leave the note?" I asked.

"On the coffee table under your anniversary gift. See?" We both looked at the table. "Well, what do you think about that? We've been robbed!"

"The purrfect crime, no doubt," I said, pointing to a small furry mouse lying on that table.

"Uh oh. Klepto-Kitty's been at it again. She looked so innocent with those big, baby blues and that beguiling siren song of hers. I swear I had no idea she was a cat burglar."

"Ella, did you purr-loin my husband's

love note?" The adorable kitten blinked at me and made the sweet sounds to which Jack had referred. Part purr and part meow, they were sweetly charming. She flopped over on her side, and then rolled over onto her back.

"Paws up! I'd say that's a confession, my love. We'll have to add shiny objects to the list of her temptations." Ella's life of crime had started with my warm, wooly socks. One by one, they had begun to disappear. Then one evening I caught her running down the hall with my knitted scarf trailing behind her as she straddled it awkwardly. From there she had moved onto ribbons and bows, delighting in removing them from wedding presents that arrived in the mail.

"Well, it can't have gone far. I don't have nearly as much turf to cover as I do at home to find her secret hideaways. I'm dying for coffee, but I want my anniversary present. I like shiny objects, too." I dashed over to the coffee table and did a careful search of the area around it. When I got down on my knees to peer under the table and furniture, I had help. Two cats in a slightly spooked mode, peered under the furniture as though something might jump out at them any minute.

"Miles, if you know where Mommy's pretty present is, you'd better tell me."

"Yes, an accessory to the theft of an accessory. That will go down in the annals of feline crime." Jack wore a big smile as he poured coffee from a jug into mugs. The aroma was intoxicating.

"Aha," I said reaching under a club chair to retrieve Jack's note. When I sat up to read it, Jack was smiling as he bit into a delicious looking tart. Le Petite Patisserie has the most scrumptious *pâte sablée* with fillings that blissfully celebrate the flavors of French Polynesia. Tahitian vanilla, coconut, as well as more exotic tropical fruit flavors. An unrepentant chocoholic, my favorite is filled with chocolate ganache topped with a thin layer of passion fruit Bavarian cream, then drizzled with a tangy passion fruit syrup. Jack dangled the box of pastries.

"I have to read my love note first, darling." I read it aloud.

"Roses are red; violets are blue. Gone for sweets and coffee, too. Here's a little bauble as a token of my affection. A beautiful pearl, that's no match for your perfection. Your grateful and loving husband of one full week."

"You have to admit. It started out well. Sort of lost the rhythm and rhyme after that."

"It's lovely, Jack." I stood up and went to plant a kiss on that sweet man's lips. "You did not buy me that black pearl and diamond pendant, did you?"

"I did. I caught that sparkle in your eye when you saw it. I can't resist that any more than I can withstand the siren song of little miss sticky paws over there."

"It was way too expensive, Jack."

"I'm flush, now that your boss has picked up the tab for our honeymoon."

"I should say it's the thought that counts, but that pendant is a beauty. I'm going to find it and give Ella back that furry mouse she left behind as a clue to her villainy. Wish me luck," I took several sips of coffee and left for our bedroom. I had learned a few things about where Ella hid her booty.

"Happy hunting. While we're on the subject of stolen jewelry you probably won't be surprised to hear that a passenger has reported another theft."

"Aha! So, you did do a little detecting

while you were out and about," I hollered over my shoulder as I stepped into our bedroom. Jack murmured something in reply, but by then I was in the closet moving suitcases and checking the pockets that weren't zippered shut.

"Ta-da!" I called out a few minutes later. I went bounding back into the sitting room dangling that trophy. "They ought to put me to work finding that jewel thief. I'd have the case solved like that!" I snapped my fingers. Then I did a little dance of triumph, borrowing a couple moves from the dancers that had entertained us the night before. The smirk on Jack's face fled when I added a beguiling wifely smile to my routine

"Put that pearl in here for safe keeping," Jack said handing me the little black box in which he had bought that pendant. I did as he asked. Then Jack pulled me to him and kissed me like a one-week-husband ought to kiss a one-week-wife. I laughed as he snuffled my hair.

"This marriage has turned out to be one of my brightest ideas ever, don't you agree?" I ran my hand along the side of his face. Jack clutched it in his, placing a light kiss on my palm.

"Your idea? As I recall, I'm the one who proposed. I would have done it that first night at dinner or the next day except I was afraid it would spook you. Not to mention you were still on the list of suspects in a murder investigation. It's hardly proper police procedure to propose marriage to a suspect."

"I'm free and clear now, copper. What are you going to do about it?" Miles interrupted that inquiry with a plaintive cry. The hair on the back of my neck stood up.

"What on earth, Miles?"

That's when the screams began. Followed by a splash.

2 OSCAR! OSCAR! OSCAR!

The screaming came in bursts followed by shouts of "man overboard," just like in a movie. Jack and I ran for the veranda as soon as we heard that splash. An eerie silence hovered in the wake of those screams.

"I don't see anything, do you, Jack?" Our cabin was aft, with our large veranda affording us an excellent view of the ocean on this side of the ship. Of course, we were moving through the water at a steady clip, so it was hard to say where we ought to be looking for anyone who had fallen overboard.

"Not a thing. Maybe it's a false alarm," Jack said. Before I could respond, a call went out over the loudspeaker.

OSCAR! OSCAR! OSCAR!

"No false alarm, Georgie—that's the call to muster the crew."

Jack and I both scanned the ocean for any sign of a person floundering in the water that rippled as our ship passed through it. It was a long way down from our location on one of the upper decks. Above us was the pool deck. At this end of the ship, that area was devoted to adults only. Next to that was a fitness facility with a running track open to views of the surrounding ocean. I was pleasantly surprised that we weren't disturbed by noise from the busy areas above us.

"I can't imagine how someone fell overboard, can you? The rails are high, and there are warnings not to climb or sit on them even here in the adult section of the ship."

"It does happen, despite all the warnings. A little early in the morning for a mishap by someone who's had too much to drink."

"Unless the party started last night and it's still going. Is the ship slowing?" I asked.

"Yes. We've probably already moved a mile or more past the point where we were when we heard that first scream. The search has begun already. See?" Jack nodded in the direction of a small launch that had swept into view.

OSCAR! OSCAR! OSCAR! I shuddered as that call went out again.

"Why run alongside the ship, Jack, since we've moved past the point where the incident occurred?"

"I presume they have launches heading away from the ship, too. No doubt, toward some marker or buoy, dropped at the location where the person went overboard. Maybe they're trying to get a better understanding of where or how someone fell into the water based on the report they got from the witness. Jumped, more likely. As you pointed out, these ships are built to avoid accidents."

"Suicide? How awful!" I exclaimed.

"I suppose it's also possible they're checking to make sure the jumper didn't get snagged on something jutting out at the water line. Don't ask me what that could be. I think it's more likely that the force of the water around the ship would push away a man overboard."

"Hitting the water from even a couple of stories up has to be dangerous if not deadly. I wonder what deck that passenger was on when he fell."

"It's like hitting concrete if you fall from fifty feet up, Georgie."

"Oh, no. That's horrible."

"At least the water's not cold. If the man overboard survived the fall, there's a better chance for rescue. It doesn't take more than a few seconds to drown, though, if he was unconscious when he hit the water. Not much longer than that to disappear underwater after drowning. The ship is stopping, so I guess that means they intend to drop anchor here or circle back around." A knock on our door gave me a jolt as I considered what Jack was saying about a ship this size changing course.

"Who is it?" Jack hollered as he dashed to the door.

"Bill Tate, Jack. I need to speak to you. It's urgent."

"That's the head of security, Georgie. I introduced you to him, remember?" I nodded, smoothing my hair down as Jack opened the door. I was still wearing my silk robe and slippers. After standing on my head in the closet searching for my missing anniversary gift, I wouldn't be a bit shocked if my hair was a fright. In all the excitement, I hadn't given a moment's notice to my appearance.

"Come on in, Bill." Jack said, inviting him in and shutting the door behind him as soon as he had stepped in out of the corridor.

"Hello, Georgie."

"Nice to see you again, Bill," I said. I didn't exactly mean that, but he had such a worried expression on his face, I felt like I ought to be polite. I was curious about his visit at such an odd moment. I wasn't the only one. Our two Siamese cats were on point, sniffing his shoes, then working their way up to the cuffs of his pants. I was about to shoo them away when Bill reached down and patted Miles. Ella, more skittish, backed away until Bill stood up again.

"We've got a situation on our hands, Jack."

"Yes, we've figured that out. A passenger overboard."

"Not just that, but a murder."

I gasped before I could stop myself. "Murder?"

"I'm afraid so. The woman who let out those alarming screams is a passenger and a witness. Wendy Cutler claims three men were fighting or wrestling over something a few decks below her. Then one went overboard, another dropped to the ground, and a third took off. When we got to the location, we found a man dead, stabbed more than once—his throat cut. The only good news about all this is that we got to the scene quickly before anyone could disturb it. It's plenty disturbing already."

"Can you keep passengers away from there?"

"Yes. We've 'tented' it like we do when there's unsightly damage to a spot on board before we can dock for repairs. It's in an out of the way section of Deck 6 where there's not much foot traffic. I have a security associate posted in case someone gets curious. Passengers have started to gather on the top deck with questions about the shouts and the alert that went out after that."

"That passenger was on the ball."

"Our MOB—an automated Man

Overboard Detection System would have kicked in even without a witness. It's state of the art with motion sensors and thermal detection designed to alert the ship's bridge, stop the ship, and initiate search and rescue protocols in a situation like this one. You're right about her being on the ball, though. She called for a nearby crew member even before that guy went over the rails when she saw those men fighting, then hollered about the man overboard. Our staff person, David Engels, arrived just as he was falling and saw the passenger enter the water. He was able to corroborate the ship's data with his own. We're no longer getting a thermal reading, though— that's not good."

"Okay, so what can we do for you, Bill?"

"The Captain called headquarters to report the incident. Ari'i nui, as they say around here, is on his way. The Big Chief himself got in on it. He's on his way as we speak."

"Big Chief? You don't mean Max Marley, do you?" I felt another wave of shock wash over me as I asked that question. I'm not sure why I should have felt that way. Max takes every major setback in his company personally. The fact that Jack and I were on the ship probably made that an even bigger issue for him. Max had not only insisted on paying for our honeymoon but had stepped in for my deceased father and escorted me down the aisle at my wedding.

"Yes. Max Marley is on his way," Bill replied.

"You can't mean that literally, given his schedule. Besides, the Fantasy of the Sea won't be back in Tahiti until the day after tomorrow—mid-morning at the earliest, right?" Jack asked.

"That's our plan—to conduct a search and rescue operation, but keep to our scheduled arrival time back in Papeete. From what Captain Andrews tells me, the company's founder is planning to leave as soon as he can and intends to be in Tahiti for our return. And, Max Marley expects a full accounting of what's gone on here."

"That sounds like Max," I muttered. "He can't possibly believe all this can be wrapped up by then, can he?"

"I don't know him personally, but I have heard stories about his expectations as well as what happens when his employees don't meet them. That brings me to the reason I'm here, Jack. He suggested that I get in touch with you, right away. As you can imagine, we don't have much of a track record when it comes to dealing with a homicide. We also don't have much time before all of this might get much more complicated. Technically, we're in international waters and outside the territorial limit for the authorities in French Polynesia to get involved. Not that there's a reason to engage them yet. Captain Andrews is officially overseeing the search and rescue operation. He says we're staying put the rest of the day. Overnight, too, if necessary. Tomorrow morning, though, we'll have to make a brief stop in Bora Bora. Then we'll head back to Papeete so you and other passengers can catch your return flights as planned on Day 10 of our cruise."

"This is a U.S.-owned ship and one of the few cruise lines that fly the U.S. flag. That means U.S. authorities have jurisdiction, right?" I asked.

"Yes, but that will most likely mean the FBI, Georgie," Jack offered. "Of course, it could be more complicated than that if the murder victim or his murderer aren't U.S. citizens."

"The dead man had a U.S. driver's license on him with a Texas address. The name on it is the same as the one on his shipboard guest I.D.—Jake Nugent. A check of his credit cards, and a review of his personal profile on record with the Marvelous Marley World Cruise line, also verify he's a U.S. citizen. I've already notified the FBI."

"What about the passenger overboard?"

"That's a bit odd. No one has reported a missing person. Staff members are checking with all passengers who have gathered on the upper deck. They're also making the rounds, going cabin by cabin to account for the whereabouts of everyone on the passenger manifest. We're doing the same for staff members and the crew. That way we hope to identify the passenger that's gone overboard even if he was traveling alone. If we don't spot him in the water, that is. Drowning victims sink fast, though." Bill Tate was clearly distressed and gave me an anxious glance as he spoke those last few words.

"That's what Jack told me, Bill. I know this must be upsetting for you. I'm sorry."

"Thanks," he said. "I should prepare myself for this to get worse before it gets better with one man dead and another missing. Our eyewitness claims that the two men fighting with him pushed the man who went overboard up and over the rails. If the man has drowned, that's two murders."

"Won't the body resurface more quickly in this warm water?"

"Yes, Jack. Captain Andrews will keep patrols up nonstop, even after dark, hoping to recover the body if we're not able to rescue the passenger. By morning, we should have support from Papeete to continue the search so we can move on."

"I hope you can identify the passenger who's gone overboard. That might help us figure out who the third guy is who's still roaming around on the ship somewhere," Jack said.

"That's an awful thought, Jack, given he may have killed two men already. Aren't there cameras nearby that can help identify him?" I asked.

"Unfortunately, that's more bad news. I had someone scan the footage collected in that area at the time the dispute took place, and the passenger went overboard. We got a great look at the dead man, but no clear view of the other two men. I don't know if they knew where the camera was placed and avoided it on purpose or if they just lucked out. Mostly, it's a blur of bad guys in dark clothes."

Gone was my easy-going guy who had swept into the suite less than an hour before those blood-curdling screams. "Are you concerned that this could be an act of terrorism?" Jack asked.

My heart skipped a beat. It had crossed my mind when all the screaming began, but once that "man overboard" cry went out I'd let go of that fear. Now it was back.

"That's always an immediate concern these days when there's trouble on board. Terrorism is the biggest nightmare for security in the industry. We've notified Homeland Security and have run the scenarios we've been trained to use to sort problems. This incident looks more like a falling out among thieves, Jack."

"What makes you say that?"

"A piece of jewelry was found at the scene."

"Well, that's important. I'd like to review

whatever information you've gathered about the thefts. As soon as you can, make a copy of Jake Nugent's photo on his passenger I.D. or driver's license. Maybe the eyewitness or one of the passengers who reported the stolen jewelry can tell us something about him."

"That's a terrific idea, Jack," I said. "If he was hanging out with the other two men, maybe someone saw them together and can help I.D. the other men."

"I can email those files to you right away. I have a laptop you can use if you don't have one, or I can send them to your cell phone. You're also welcome to review the video footage from that fight on Deck 6. Maybe you'll spot something we missed." Bill bit his bottom lip. "This is an unbelievable mess. I've been in the business for almost twenty-five years. I've had to deal with shipboard crime lots of times but never anything like this. I want to get to the bottom of this quickly but without scaring the heck out of people. What do you suggest, Jack?"

"I'll take you up on the offer of the laptop. Send me all the background you have on your investigation into the jewelry thefts, along with any information about Jake Nugent.

Keep the public focus on the search and rescue efforts you're making to locate the missing passenger. At this point, that's the issue that's going to arouse curiosity and concern—especially when your guests realize how this will impact their itinerary. If I'm clear about what you've said, we're going to put into Bora Bora a day late and won't stay long enough for passengers to go ashore. Not everyone is going to be happy about that. From the standpoint of a homicide investigation, that's a break though. If passengers and crew remain on board, there's less chance for our murderous thief to become a fugitive."

"If I could do it, I'd head back without making that stop in Bora Bora. Captain Andrews tells me it's needed to restock water and other provisions for the return trip to Papeete. He'll keep the stop short and will send as few crew members ashore as possible. I'll post watches around the clock so no one can sneak off."

"In the meantime, Bill, I'll do what I can to preserve evidence from the crime scene and keep my inquiry into Jake Nugent's death as discrete as I can. No matter how reassuring you try to be, hearing about a murder on board is going to trigger concerns about terrorism. All we need is to start a panic."

I tried not to imagine what that might mean in a confined space like a cruise ship. Jennifer, my best friend who runs a travel agency, had once told me about problems on board a cruise ship when an engine failed. In that case, Jennifer said the fear that the ship was going to sink had led to an ugly situation. I hadn't seen it, but cell phone footage that passengers had shared on Facebook and other social media sites was dreadful from the way Jennifer described it.

"I suppose it's good this all happened so early when most passengers were still in their staterooms, rather than milling about on Deck 6 or elsewhere," I offered struggling to find a bright spot in the dismal situation.

"When that alarm sounded, it set off a rush of activity from passengers. Mostly a flurry of phone calls and questions for cabin stewards who were nearby. Captain Andrews acted quickly to post staff on the upper deck to answer questions about the fact that a passenger had gone overboard. No one other than Wendy Cutler has come forward as a witness to that fight or the passenger going overboard."

"The first thing I need to do is have a look at the dead man, and I'd like to speak to the first responder. We want to take photos and collect evidence before it gets contaminated or deteriorates in the heat. Did you leave the jewelry where you found it?"

"We haven't touched a thing except to put up that tent around the area. A member of our security staff, Tom Reasoner, was the first to reach the scene since he happened to be on Deck 6 already. He was there in less than two minutes after David Engels called security about the fight on Deck 6 that coincided with the loss of that passenger. When Engels mentioned the possibility that an injured passenger might be in that location, I called for the ship's doctor and ordered that tent then too. The ship's doctor is there now taking photos. Dr. Maggie Hayward's no coroner, but she did an internship or something like that during her medical training, so she understands how to collect and record necessary information. She checked the passenger for signs of life and pulled that I.D. card from his pocket so we could get a name and cabin number for him. She told me she wouldn't move anything until you arrived."

"Excellent! Um, we're going to need a

morgue—someplace cool."

"No problem. Cruise ships are required to carry body bags and to have a morgue. Murders don't often happen on board, but deaths do." Jack and Bill chatted for another minute or two and agreed to meet in ten minutes at the scene of the crime with a couple of crew members who could help move the body.

I could tell the wheels in Jack's head were turning, trying to figure out how to make do without all the supports available to him in Orange County. *Max had done the right thing to put Jack in charge*, I thought as we said goodbye to Bill.

"Get dressed, Georgie. You're coming with me."

"I am? You want me to help out at the crime scene?" I was caught off guard by the suggestion. Part of me wanted to tag along and poke my nose into the murder and mayhem. On the other hand, I don't do well with dead bodies.

"No, Dear. You're part of my cover. A happy honeymoon couple out and about on one of the last days of their romantic South Sea

Island cruise."

"I should have known I'd be a prop or a decoy. Do you want me to flash my legs to distract passers-by if they wander our way?" I lifted my skirt and pointed the toe of my slipper bending my leg like Claudette Colbert flagging down a passing car in It Happened One Night.

"I have no doubt that would work like a charm. Let's hope it doesn't come to that. I'd prefer to keep those gams of yours under wraps like the rest of this investigation."

"Good luck. None of this will remain undercover for long. Once Mad Max arrives it'll be game over, Detective."

"True. Your meddlesome boss is likely to beat us to Papeete, Georgie. Even if he uses the corporate jet and bypasses airport hassles, he can't reduce the flight time by much, especially if he stops and refuels along the way. That means many hours in the air once he files a flight plan and gets to the airport. I figure we've got 24 hours before Max Marley can have a Rumpelstiltskin tantrum on this ship or anywhere nearby."

"That's not a lot of time to solve a murder—even for you. Maybe I should contact

Max and try to head off that tantrum. I'll appeal to the importance of keeping a cool head and low profile when we arrive in Papeete. If I can call forth Max the Guardian Angel of Marvelous Marley World and tap his concern about not blemishing his brand that might take precedence over his desire to punish the bearers of bad news."

"Go for it, Georgie," Jack said handing me a cup of coffee and pouring himself another. "Knowing you, by the time he gets here he'll believe the whole cool-head-low-profile approach was his idea in the first place. Getting updates from someone he trusts will help him feel more like he has control."

"One can only hope," I said as I scarfed down that coffee and one of those delicious chocolate tarts. "What does one wear to a shipboard crime scene?" I wondered aloud.

"I'd opt for comfort. We'll make this as quick as we can, but it could take a while."

"Will do," I said as I dashed into our bedroom and slipped into a pair of black, stretchy cropped pants and a red knit boatneck top. Finally, I combed my hair, and put on a bit of mascara and lip gloss.

"Red is your color," Jack said when I reemerged moments later. He smiled appreciatively. I'm not sure whether red was my color or his, but I'd added more of it to my wardrobe since I learned how much he liked to see me in it.

"And so forgiving if you happen to have blood and gore on your itinerary. Just so you know it, I'm considering making gold or purple my new favorite color."

"No problem. You'd look just as ravishing in those colors, too." Jack swept me into his arms and kissed me. I returned the favor. "Let's go before I change my mind about getting involved in this cops and robbers mission," he said, releasing me from that embrace.

"Or before this honeymoon can get any more bizarre." I glanced over my shoulder at the underwater scene on the opposite wall. The cats had figured out how to trigger the motion detectors, and the scene was flowing again. Little Ella was dashing back and forth, chasing after a school of brightly-colored fish. Miles' head was moving rapidly as he tracked her motions, like a sports fan at a tennis match. "At least the cats are having a good time," I said knowing full well the game afoot for us was not tennis.

3 PASSENGER X

"We've done a complete census, and we're not missing a passenger, Sir," the young man said as his gaze wandered to the tented area from which Jack and Bill had just emerged. When we first arrived on Deck 6, I had followed Jack in there, but I hadn't stayed long. The blood was more than I could handle. Besides, it was crowded. Tom Reasoner, waiting at the scene, had gone over what he found when he arrived at the site, and what he had done since then. He repeated much of the story Bill had told us in our suite, but this time with show and tell. Gruesome.

Jack inspected the identification card Dr. Maggie Hayward had retrieved from Jake Nugent's pocket. It was now in a small plastic bag. Dr. Hayward, who asked that we call her Maggie, had brought plastic bags with her from the infirmary along with latex gloves, tweezers, and a few other items. Jack slipped on a pair of those latex gloves and began to inspect the area.

Bill took photos as Jack or Maggie pointed out one thing or another—including a bloody shoe print. Scrapes and scuff marks on the rail suggested there had been a scuffle before that passenger went overboard.

"What's that, Jack?" I had asked pointing to something snagged on an exposed edge of the rail.

"I'm not sure," Jack said as he had Bill take a photo before using a gloved hand to slip it into a plastic bag. He held it up. "It's a piece of plastic, I think, Georgie."

"I have a magnifying examination lamp in the infirmary. We can take a closer look. At these, too," Maggie said as she lifted two blond hairs from the body lying on the deck in a pool of blood. That's when I began to feel the need to escape.

"Can you get a picture of this, please, Bill?" Bill leaned in close and snapped a photo of a necklace partly hidden by the dead man's body. After Bill snapped a picture or two, Jack lifted the body a little and slid that necklace the rest of the way out of a pocket where it must have been before the man fell. Bill shot more pictures as Jack held aloft an elaborate piece of jewelry that combined braided gold with gems of various colors. As he slipped it into a plastic bag, I spoke up.

"I've seen that necklace before," I said.

"Was it worn by a cool blond with shoulder length hair?" Jack asked.

"If I can clear my head, I might be able to remember," I replied. When I peered more closely, I got a better look at the necklace. Unfortunately, when Jack had lifted the body to pick up that necklace, I also got a better view of a savage wound that must have caused the man's death. That's when I had abandoned Jack and the others, leaving them in that little tent of horrors.

"What I can tell you is that it's a fake," I said as I fled.

As soon as I drew in a couple of deep breaths of sea air, my memory of that necklace came back to me. The woman wearing it was no blond. A sultry brunette with dark eyes set off by smoky eye makeup and wearing dark red lipstick. Men surrounded her as she stood in a lounge area waiting for the maître d' to seat her for dinner. She spoke with great animation and apparent ease.

Had that dead man been among them? I strained to recall the appearance of each of the men with her that evening. That scene in the tent still had me shook up. At this point, I couldn't even be sure I remembered how many men had been in that circle of admirers.

I gave up and composed a message to Max. When I sent that message, I hoped the "angel Max" rather than the "devil Max" would be on the receiving end. My boss who avowed he possessed those two warring personas, was as chimerical as the fantasies spun by the entertainment conglomerate he had founded decades ago. In his 70s, Maximillian Marley showed no signs of relinquishing his leadership role anytime soon. While I was still pondering the fate of my text message to Max, a member of Bill's security team showed up in his spiffy white uniform. That's when we learned that we had a man overboard but not a single missing passenger.

"What about the crew?" Jack asked after Adam delivered his message about the passenger census.

"All present and accounted for, Sir."

"Thanks, Adam," Bill said. That sounded like a dismissal to me, but Adam lingered scanning the deck, glancing side-to-side.

"Sir, is this the point at which Passenger X went overboard?"

"Passenger X?" I asked.

"Yes. That's how we're referring to the missing passenger until we have a cabin number or name to use."

I scrutinized the young man who was shifting from one foot to another. Perhaps he was anxious about the missing person report he had just delivered to his boss, the Security Chief, Bill Tate. A missing passenger at sea was bad enough. Not being able to account for the person's identity had to be much worse.

Does he know more about all that has gone on here on Deck 6 than has been shared publicly? I wondered. Despite the hope to handle the homicide investigation discretely, it seemed unlikely that a murder could be kept from the crew, even if they could conceal such information from passengers. Is that what had him so antsy? There was one way to find out.

"Adam, is there something bothering you?" I asked. He glanced at me and then his eyes flitted Jack's way before settling on Bill's face.

"We had an incident near this spot the night before last. A steward broke up a confrontation and reported it as a dispute between passengers who'd had too much to drink."

"That's good to know. Do you have a record of the passengers who were involved in the incident?" Jack asked.

"We don't have their names. The steward didn't call security to the scene but filed an incident report later. The reason I remembered it now isn't just that it happened near here, but one of the passengers the steward spoke to didn't have a ship-issued identity card with him. He claimed he'd left it in his cabin. When he filed the report later, the steward made an offhand comment. Something like, 'how did he get that drunk if he didn't have his I.D. card with him at the bar?' I assumed the guy fighting with him must have bought the drinks before they went at it. What if the guy without an I.D. card is Passenger X?"

"Since he didn't have I.D., did the steward include the passenger's cabin number in the report?"

"Yes, Bill. He also offered to escort the passenger back to his cabin, but he declined the offer of assistance. They seemed to have settled their differences, so the steward let it go at that point."

"Jack, if you can handle the investigation here, I think Adam and I should go check out the cabin this guy claimed was his. Maybe the incidents are unrelated. It's also possible that it involved a disagreement between two of our three thieves. Maybe already fighting as their scheme unraveled. It's a shame that steward didn't call security, though. We would have scanned the card for the passenger carrying an I.D. to confirm his identity. And, we would have insisted that the passenger without I.D. take us to his cabin to retrieve it."

"There's another thing. Bill. I already checked the passenger manifest. The passenger occupying the stateroom with the number recorded on that incident report is a woman traveling alone. I'm guessing that drunken passenger was out of it or just picked a cabin at random hoping to get the steward off his back."

"The point of issuing those electronic I.D. cards is so that sort of thing can't happen," Bill said, sighing deeply. He ran a hand up the back of his neck. "Let's go have a talk with the woman in that cabin."

"If you're lucky, that number wasn't random, even if that's what the unidentified passenger intended."

"I hope you're right, Jack. I'm not looking forward to needlessly hassling an already hassled guest."

Bill was right to be concerned about adding to a guest's distress. In the short distance from our suite to the tented area, Jack and I had heard grumbling from passengers. Some were disappointed. Others were scared, but some were angry too.

So far, passengers had only heard a brief announcement that the search for a missing passenger would delay arrival at the next port of call, Bora Bora. A more formal briefing would be provided later in the afternoon. The details weren't likely to make passengers any happier unless the search and rescue teams located Passenger X by then.

"I have a question before you go," Jack said. "Could you have a stowaway? Security was tight in Papeete when we went through customs before boarding, but it seemed more casual in Moorea and other stops. Can new passengers or crew members come aboard when you put into port? Could someone have done that without your knowing about it?"

"We're paranoid about stowaways–especially since 9/11. It's not just that we're worried about terrorism. Our supply officers try to account for everything and everyone that comes or goes on this ship. That minimizes theft. The kitchen commissary and galley workers are obsessive about the handling of provisions, especially the sort of fresh produce, meat, or seafood that would come aboard at a stop along the way. They monitor the transfer of goods and even have protocols for getting rid of the containers in which goods are delivered to the dock. Food-borne illness is a bigger threat than terrorism, day-to-day. Along the way, the Chef usually buys fresh items from purveyors he trusts. He places those orders ahead of our arrival in port, so he knows who's going to pick up or drop off merchandise."

"Sounds like the way we worry about the chain of custody when it comes to handling evidence. What about other supplies?"

"At the start of a cruise, items like linens, cleaning products, toiletries, and paper products are stocked for the entire itinerary. Sometimes supply officers guess wrong and need to pick up items ashore. Given we're on the last leg of our cruise, maybe the protocol was relaxed at our last stop, but I'd be surprised if a breach went unnoticed. We can ask the supply officer, but Chef Gerard is most likely to have made pickups along the way. I'll start with him."

"I can do that, if you'd like, Bill. Gerard and I are old friends from culinary school." Bill was pondering my offer, perhaps wondering how much he ought to engage a passenger like me in the business of investigating a shipboard crime. He was being pulled in a lot of directions at once, however, even with Jack's help.

"I'd take her up on that offer, Bill. She's a vetted company associate, like you are, with management experience in food service and public relations. If Gerard has concerns about anything that's happened on this cruise, he'll have no trouble telling Georgie about it. Chef

Gerard is the only man on this ship who's allowed to send my wife sweet nothings. He seems trustworthy even though he's aware of Georgie's weakness and not afraid to exploit it," Jack said, raising an eyebrow as he tried to lighten up the unhappy mood that had settled upon us.

"Weakness? What's that?" Bill asked still in a bit of a fog.

"Chocolate!" Jack and I said in unison. That broke the spell, and the Security Chief laughed for the first time since he had stepped into our cabin earlier this morning.

"If you can do anything to expedite the investigation, Georgie, that would be great. Not to mention that since you're dealing with an old friend, you can impose upon him to keep matters quiet."

"Understood," I said. I was relieved at the thought of getting away from Deck 6, even if it meant poking my nose into affairs below deck. It would be interesting to see how this floating city fed the legions on board. Not just passengers but all the staff that it took to serve them.

I'd been taken on a quick tour of the

galley when we used the reservations Max had made for us in one of the ship's two premiere dining spots, Neptune's Garden. Gerard, a Michelin-starred chef, was quite the showman. The food was exquisite—more Mediterranean than South Seas—with an appropriate emphasis on the freshest seafood. A gorgeous display with an ice carving of a mermaid had greeted us at dinner that night.

"Even if I don't come up with information about a breach of protocol or a stowaway, I'm going to see if Gerard can cook up some event for tonight. The last night on board is usually a special one, but an extra culinary extravaganza might take some of the edge off passengers' disappointment about not arriving in Bora Bora today as planned."

"That's an excellent idea. A word of caution about the need to continue to be discrete. Not just to avoid disturbing the passengers any further. As much as I hate to say it if someone did get on board without a ticket, they most likely had help from an insider." That worried expression Adam had worn suddenly made sense. The one Bill now wore was almost identical.

Maybe I shouldn't be quite so eager to

play sleuth, even with an old friend like Chef Gerard, I thought as I bid farewell to my husband who had made the transition from honeymooner to detective. He was one step away from telling me to go back to our suite and leave the sleuthing to the pros.

"Don't do anything I wouldn't do, Sweetheart," he whispered using his hokey Philip Marlowe voice. My one-week-husband, who looked much more like James Garner in the Rockford Files than Humphrey Bogart, had learned a thing or two. I'm not a woman who's easily deterred once my mind is made up, so he hadn't tried to stop me.

"You can count on me to play it cool, Pal." Food didn't sound that bad now that I was out in the fresh sea air instead of in that tent. "If I score some five-star chow, I'll share it with you, handsome," I whispered. My wise-cracking dame voice was even hokier than Jack's impression of the classic film noir detective. Thank goodness no one could hear it.

"Gerard says you should meet him in the galley on Deck 2. Do you know how to get there or do you want an escort?" Bill asked. Yielding to the worried expressions on the men's faces, I opted for an escort even though I felt quite sure

I could find my way to that galley on my own. The dead man couldn't hurt me, nor could the man overboard, but that third man was another story. Who was the ruthless slasher? Where had he gone? Was he still lurking about or watching us from a deck above us? I was suddenly very grateful that I had an escort.

4 THE COMMISSARY

"Georgie, Darling! How are you? Did you come to pitch in? Are you hungry?" The thin, energetic man in a tall chef's hat rushed toward me as he peppered me with those questions. The galley on Deck 2 where passengers could avail themselves of a nonstop buffet had to be the busiest kitchen on the ship.

The kitchen staff served breakfast all day, adding other items for lunch, afternoon tea, and dinner. The kitchen was probably the largest one on the ship but appeared to be a more compact version of what you'd find in a restaurant or hotel. The place was buzzing with activity. Steam was billowing from pots on the stove and from a water bath used to keep containers of food warm until a runner transported them to one of the buffet stations in Kehlani's Lagoon. A rich medley of aromas swirled amid those vapors. Expediters shouted for items needed out on the serving line or relayed a special request from a guest.

A cacophony of clinking, clanging, scraping, and chopping sounds issued from every corner of the busy kitchen. It was music to my ears! Nostalgia rushed through me, filling me with memories of the excitement I first felt when I had become a chef decades earlier.

Kitchens are noisy places, especially in the confined space of a ship's galley—even one as large as this one that served hundreds of passengers each day. Mega ships fed many more meals to hungry diners. The newest ship in Max Marley's fleet, the Marvelous Marley World—MMW Fantasy of the Sea, is a midsize luxury liner with just under a thousand passengers on board. Max had opted not to go the "ultra-luxury" route with his cruise line, hoping to keep fares affordable enough to attract the families that had made Marvelous Marley World a household name.

"I was hoping you might show me around if you have time. I know there are a dozen kitchens throughout the ship, and I've only seen one of them. I'm curious too about the storage and preparation areas you mentioned."

"To be exact, there are fourteen full-sized kitchens, plus six smaller galley areas with minimal food service for burgers and fries, salads and sandwiches, or coffee and pastries—like Le Petite Patisserie that you enjoy so much."

"Those staging areas look a lot like what you see at a food court or Starbucks," I said.

"Exactly! This kitchen is bigger than the one you've already seen, but they're all similar in layout. Working in a smaller space has become old hat to me now. A trickier issue for me was getting used to relying on electric heat since no open flame is allowed on the ship. As you can imagine, fear of a fire on board is huge!"

"I'll take your word for it rather than even think of such a thing, Gerard."

"Would you like to go below to the commissary kitchen and storage area to see how we manage to stash food away for a ten-day voyage like the one you're on?"

"Yes! That would be wonderful, Gerard."

"Hang on a second. Paolo, will you come here please?"

"Yes, Chef. What is it?" The man who bounded our way wore a hat slightly shorter than Gerard's. As in many kitchens, Gerard as the Executive Chef wore the tallest hat. Even in the shorter hat, Paolo towered over Gerard and me.

"Paolo, this is my friend, Georgie Shaw—Director of the Food & Beverage Division at Marvelous Marley World. Meet my Sous Chef, Paolo Vannetti. I snatched him away from a delightful bistro in Tuscany a few years ago. He's responsible for adding more Mediterranean flare to our menus." I shook the hand of the attractive Italian man with blue eyes and blond hair. He spoke to Gerard even though his eyes were on me.

"You are too kind, Chef. It was a great opportunity for me to join the Marvelous World of Marley. I am pleased to meet you, Ms. Shaw."

"Nice to meet you, too, Paolo. At Marvelous Marley World, it's first names only, so please call me Georgie." He beamed a broad smile and bowed a little. "As you wish, Georgie. How can I be of service, Chef?"

"I'm leaving you in charge while I show Georgie around."

"Ciao!" Paolo did another of those slight bows as Gerard took off.

"Follow me! You have questions about how we run the kitchens on the ship, don't you?"

Thank goodness Jack had suggested I dress for comfort. I felt sure I was about to get a workout. I took a couple of extra steps to catch up with Gerard. Before I could reply, Gerard dashed off and spoke to a woman dressed as one of the expediters we had been introduced to in the galley kitchen at Neptune's Garden. She nodded and then tore off on some mission. Gerard was on the move again.

"Yes. I'd love to hear how you handle the need for fresh food and other supplies without the daily access available to luxury hotels and restaurants ashore. Guests must expect a similar level of service. I take that for granted, although I've only been on a few short excursions before this one."

"Yes, they do expect quality and service,

although we cater to lots of families who are more used to eating on the run. They're also more forgiving than the high-end clients I served on the ultra-luxury line where I used to work. For the most part, families expect standard fare like burgers, steaks, chicken, pizza, and spaghetti. We serve food kids will eat. Of course, we accommodate our more adventurous eaters at Neptune's Garden or The Captain's Table. I know you've had a chance to sample the cuisine at both places."

"That's true, and it's fabulous. Room service has also been fantastic when we've been too lazy to leave our cabin."

"Lazy? Okay, if that's what you want to call it," he smirked. I felt a blush rising on my cheeks.

"Stop it, Gerard. This whole married woman thing is still new for me. I haven't identified the appropriate euphemisms to use quite yet." Gerard guffawed.

"You are a hoot, Georgie Shaw. I can't believe I can still make you blush! I used to be quite good at that with my use of colorful language. I've never relied on euphemisms as you know."

"You were one of my earliest tutors in 'kitchen French,' and I admit it was a little hard to take at first. I suppose I was more easily shocked than most twenty-somethings." I shrugged.

"Say no more. I remember the sad circumstances that led you to culinary school instead of finishing college. After what you'd been through, it's no wonder you were sensitive to my crudeness. At least you went back to finish college while I roamed Europe in pursuit of that Michelin Star. Funny how I ended up back at Marvelous Marley World so many years after our internship." It was Gerard who shrugged his shoulders after that comment. "You married the police detective you met during a murder investigation. That must mean you're less easily shocked now, though."

"One can only hope," I muttered as I considered the current circumstances in which I found myself. "It has been one thing after another since Jack and I met. Now, even on our honeymoon, a passenger goes missing. Have you been through this before?" Gerard came to an abrupt stop in front of an elevator in a corridor outside the kitchen. He hit the call button as he responded to my question.

"Not since I began to work for Mad Max's Marvelous Marley World of Fantasy Sea Cruises!"

"You call him Mad Max, too?" My mouth gaped open in surprise. That smirk was back on Gerard's face.

"Got you again, didn't I? It's no secret that the boss is fabulously, flamingly mad at times. It's one of the reasons I took this job. I love how over-the-top the guy can be! Where else could I work on a cruise that features Catmmando Tom's Grotto Hideaway for kids to explore? With options to dress up like Catmmando Tom complete with an eye patch and whiskers, or float around in a pool as a Merry Mermaid in water that changes color?"

The elevator door popped open, and Gerard used a keycard to activate the buttons that would take us to the commissary below. "How about audio-animatronic dolphins to ride?" He said as he leaned against the elevator rail that was one arm of a giant octopus positioned in a back corner of the elevator. Another arm snaked around behind me.

"Max does have a vivid imagination," I said eying the rather diabolical looking octopus hovering above us with one eyebrow raised along with a fiendish grin. Kids loved to hate the wild-eyed Olly-Olly Octopus, known for his skilled use of camouflage to try to trick the brave and wily Neptune's Warriors. Like Wile E. Coyote's misguided attempts to trick the Road Runner, it always ended up badly for Olly-Olly. "If you don't mind my asking, does everyone who visits the kitchen commissary and storage areas use keycards?"

"Well, they don't all have keycards like mine that work on the elevators used by guests. In places we store goods, we restrict access to ship's personnel only. Unless they're senior staff members like me, they can only enter those areas using elevators reserved for crew members. No passengers allowed! Except when we escort a passenger on a tour like the one we're taking now. That's not so different from backstage access in Arcadia Park. It keeps guest elevators free and reduces pilfering since there are fewer entry and exit points. Although it's not like you're going to take a bunch of raw steaks with you back to your crew quarters. Remember that guy Sammy who got caught boosting steaks?"

"Gosh, that was awful, wasn't it?" The elevator pinged and the doors opened.

"Awful funny, as I recall. Sammy tripped over his trousers as he tried to get away from security. Those steaks were heavier than he figured and his belt was no match for that extra weight!" We stepped out of the elevator into a cavernous space. Silver doors that I recognized as entrances to walk-in refrigerators lined one wall.

"Things sure have changed since then, haven't they?" Gerard asked with a wistful tone in his voice. "Especially after 9/11. It's no longer just worries about theft by employees. Max Marley pays the highest wages in the industry so you don't hear about as many problems as they have on other ships where they pack crew members into cramped quarters—like sardines. And pay wages that would barely keep minnows alive. Still, contamination by indifferent or disgruntled employees is a concern, so we take as many precautions as we can."

"That's true in the parks and resorts, too. We have become more security conscious everywhere. How secure are these areas? Especially when you're restocking at one of the smaller islands?" Gerard looked at me and then glanced over his shoulder.

"Not perfect, but the best in the industry as far as I can tell." He studied my face for a moment before going on with our tour.

"Those are temperature controlled walk-ins with temps that vary depending on what we have stored in them. We don't mix meat, produce, or dairy. Dry goods are kept separate, too." Gerard pointed to tall shelves like you might see in a big box store, with labeled containers indicating the contents. "At the beginning of the voyage, this entire space is packed. It's thinned out since we're nearing the end of the cruise. We always carry extra provisions in case something happens and we need to skip a port of call or end up spending an extra day at sea. Or more, maybe?" He glanced at me as though I might have additional information about changes in our itinerary.

Hmm, I wondered. *Who's trying to get information from whom?* "You're way ahead of me on what it means to have a passenger lost at sea, Chef, although I have heard we're at anchor overnight." Gerard moved to one of the large stainless steel doors before picking up the conversation again. I followed him.

"That's what I hear too. We won't delay

our return to Tahiti on this trip even though the search will push back our arrival at our last port of call. That means we'll be later than expected but won't skip Bora Bora altogether. I have a special order waiting for me for our luau that we'll now hold the last night on board. I had planned to do that beachside tonight—with a real kalua pig cooked in an imu pit. I'm going to have to cook the pig some other way, though, and we'll have to hold the luau up on deck. No dramatic dancers juggling torches," Gerard said in a frustrated tone as he opened the door to one of the refrigerators that was bigger than a large walk-in closet. He pointed to a rectangular package that took up an entire shelf.

"Voila! The pig! We'll cook up some pork roasts, beef ribs, and teriyaki chicken, too, to make sure that we have enough for the turnout we expect on the last night of a cruise," Gerard stepped into the walk-in fridge. When I followed him inside, he let the door slam shut behind us.

"About your earlier question, Georgie. I've had my suspicions that something odd is going on."

5 SHIPBOARD EXTRAVAGANZAS

"Odd? How?" I asked.

"I don't know. I found items shoved around down here, and no one was willing to admit they did it or knew what had happened. A few things turned up missing or damaged. Nothing expensive. That's part of why this seemed so odd. The pricey stuff like caviar, truffles, foie gras, and expensive bottles of wine or liqueur I use for cooking I keep in a safe in my cabin."

"Could someone have been looking for something?"

"That's possible, but what? When no one claimed to know anything, I checked the log and accounted for entries and exits as well as I could. They checked out—for the most part."

"What does that mean?"

"There is so much coming and going even during the late shifts, it's hard to be entirely sure who was where when. Crew members are supposed to keep their keycards with them always, and they are not allowed to share them with others. I couldn't prove it, but I suspected not all galley staff were following those rules. It's not surprising that in the middle of a rush one employee might ask another to run down and pick up something. Why lend out your keycard? Things happen, I guess," Gerard said.

"Did you report any of this to Bill Tate?"

"Not directly, but I filed incident reports—twice—when I couldn't get to the bottom of the matter on my own. After one of those incidents, items down here weren't just out of place, but oil had been spilled on the floor as though there might have been a shoving match and stuff got knocked down. Flour too. I threw out the dented, leaky can I found on a shelf and a bag of flour that had split open. I could tell someone had made a stab at cleaning it up. In fact, a member of the commissary kitchen staff eventually admitted he'd cleaned up the spills but swore he found it that way. He was so uncomfortable about it. Why, if he didn't do it? Maybe he was just embarrassed that he'd been so clumsy and made such a mess. It didn't seem like a big enough deal to write the guy up, so I left his name out of the report I filed. We're talking about a few dollars' worth of ingredients—no big deal."

"Gerard, why are you so wary?" Even in the privacy of the walk-in that was now growing rather cold, he did a quick side-to-side scan and lowered his voice before going on.

"Because the next morning after I had filed the second report, I found a raw duck on a cart outside my door. It had a note stuck to it with a knife. 'Chef Gerard, you don't want to run 'a fowl' of the wrong people. Quit giving your staff the 3rd degree over nothing.' I laughed at first, figuring it was a practical joke. I have been known to do such things myself, Georgie. Then when that guy went overboard this morning after a fight of some kind, it didn't seem so funny anymore."

"You heard there was a fight?"

"Yes. I was out on deck when the screaming and shouting began. Women were screaming, and one was shouting 'he pushed him over the rail,' or something like that." A chill ran through me that had nothing to do with the frigid temperature of our surroundings.

"Are you saying that more than one person was shouting and screaming?"

"Yes. I heard at least two distinct women's voices." Gerard seemed puzzled. "What do you know that I don't, Georgie?"

"You cannot tell anyone else about this, Gerard, except Bill—and Jack. Before I asked Bill to track you down so we could meet, there was a report that a fight contributed to that passenger falling overboard. That report came from one woman who screamed and alerted the crew—not two." Gerard stared at me with a penetrating gaze, almost like my super-perceptive Siamese cat, Miles. Under pressure, I gave away more details. "She mentioned that fight didn't end well for another passenger, either." Gerard's eyes widened. I changed the subject, hastily. Why add to his fearfulness with details about a murder on Deck 6?

"Gerard, why didn't you report your concerns about the previous incidents to security today, or tell them what you heard when you were up on deck?"

"I assumed they heard the screaming and that anyone that upset would have gone to the nearest staff member right away. Maybe the dead duck thing was a prank, Georgie. I don't want to get a reputation for being a whack job. It's uncomfortable, to say the least, to suspect the people around you of being up to no good without any real proof."

I flashed on my reaction when there had been a murder at Catmmando Mountain. It had been inconceivable to me that anyone with whom I worked could have done such a thing. Even when someone tried to frame me for the murder, I had a hard time seeing my coworkers as villains.

"I get it. You do need to share this with Bill, Gerard. He needs to go over all of this with you, starting at the beginning. He speaks highly of you, and will not consider you a whack job, especially under the circumstances."

"Well, if that duck prank wasn't a prank, it's more than a little scary, isn't it?" I nodded in agreement.

"Even more reason to get this on the record with Bill. Who knew you had filed those incident reports?"

"I questioned members of the galley kitchen staff who had been on duty on the occasions when I noticed a problem down here. The commissary kitchen staff, too, that had late night shifts. They all knew I was going to file an incident report. I asked the guy who had tried to clean up the mess to come to me, first, if it happened again so he wouldn't get mixed up with whatever had gone on. Paolo was there. He can tell you who all was in the room. Since he does more direct supervision than I do, he should have a better idea about kitchen staff who have had problems on the job." I shivered. This time from the cold. Gerard noticed.

"Let's get out of here before you freeze to death. Let me finish showing you around. Then, I have a surprise for you in my cabin." Gerard said raising both eyebrows, morphing back into clown mode as we stepped out of that walk-in fridge. The storage room that was also cool felt balmy by comparison to that meat locker.

"What kind of surprise?" I asked. "I'm well-aware of your practical jokes that aren't always so funny, by the way. Like when you lit that poor buffet runner's apron strings on fire on his way out to the dining room." Gerard whooped.

"He made a quick turnaround, didn't he? I had no idea the guy could move that fast!"

"You're lucky you didn't get kicked out of your internship at Marvelous Marley World for that. If guests in the dining room had seen those fiery apron strings, you could have created an uproar. Or worse—a panic with people screaming 'fire' and running for the exits!"

"I know, Georgie. I do have some bad-prank-Karma coming to me, don't I? I'm way more mature now than I was when we were in our twenties. It's not that kind of surprise, promise. Besides, passengers seem plenty upset about the missing man. I'm not interested in doing anything to rock the boat!" I rolled my eyes at the corny use of that phrase.

"Ha ha, Gerard. No one wants to make this situation worse. It's not pleasant to think about some poor man floating around out there—if he's still alive."

"Certainly, not the sort of thing you want to deal with on your cruise to paradise. Many of the conversations I've overheard have been dreadful. Not always oozing with concern for the missing man, I might add. You'd think they'd notice that their kids are standing there with eyes as big as saucers and their mouths hanging open, listening to the nasty tone and offensive language. Some of those parents ought to have their mouths washed out with soap."

"Their kids won't blush as easily as I did as a newbie in the kitchen, huh?" Gerard burst into laughter again.

"Hopefully our luau will rekindle the aloha spirit. We'll have entertainment, too. Perroquet and Penelope will sing their little ditty on a mock beach since the real one will be off limits." Then Gerard sprang into motion swinging his hips in a kind of hula meets the twist. He belted out the first line of that duet by a mermaid and a parrot:

"We live a tiki-tiki life in a teeny-tiny hut
On a strip of sandy beach near a brightly-colored reef!"

At that point, Gerard pointed to me. I couldn't pretend I didn't know the routine. We had done it many times years before as coworkers during our internship at Marvelous

Marley World. I took my cue, stepped next to Gerard, and went into action. Dancing and singing my part.

"It's an easy-peasy life full of fish and coconut
By lagoons of blue-green water where work is always brief!"

"Brief? It's almost nothing atoll—atoll—get it?" Gerard retorted adding a bit of squawk to his voice.

"Yes, I get it Perroquet!" Standing there with my hands on my hips like Princess Penelope, I abruptly ended our little routine with a question.

"Be honest, Gerard. Do you hate this song as much as I do? The idea of an oversized parrot and a petite mermaid dancing on a French Polynesian beach just irks me somehow."

"The tune does stick with you long after you wish it would leave your head. However, that is absolutely information you should not have divulged, Georgie Shaw. I now know how to torment you anytime I please. Not to mention blackmail! What would Mad Max say if he knew how you felt about Penelope and

Perroquet's tiki-tiki song?"

"Oh, go ahead. Do your worst," I said, putting my hands back on my hips. "I grew up with three brothers, so it won't be easy to torment me! And, I don't mind telling Max to his face that he missed the mark with that little ditty. Can you imagine having to play that tune, over and over, for a five-year-old smitten with the idea of Princess Penelope from Neptune's Enchanted Underwater Kingdom? Where's that parrot come from anyway? There aren't any parrots on atolls!"

Gerard was laughing at my rant as we headed across the storage space and through a pair of swinging doors into the commissary kitchen. Unlike the empty storage area, this room was buzzing with activity. The staff was busy working on large stainless steel tables. On one near us, a young man was cracking eggs into a large container, holding two eggs at a time in each hand. Crack, open, empty. Grab four more eggs and repeat! Prep work I had done many times to have enough eggs ready to scramble for a buffet. Others chopped fruits or vegetables. A man washed heads of lettuce in a large stainless steel sink, while a young woman wearing plastic gloves wrapped bacon around water chestnuts or pineapple chunks, stuck them with a toothpick, and then placed them on a large sheet pan.

"Yum, rumaki," I mumbled realizing that I was getting hungry.

"Only one of the many 'pupus' for our luau. We're having those little barbecue ribs, coconut scallop ceviche, beef teriyaki skewers, chicken mango kabobs, crispy prawns, and..."

"Please, stop! I take back what I said about being able to withstand your torment. Not that you're playing fair. One of the things I wanted to ask you about was whether you'd considered creating a spectacle of some kind for tonight. You know, something extra for passengers who are disappointed about the change in itinerary and distressed about the missing passenger? Now I'm too hungry to talk about food. Besides, that luau you have planned for tomorrow night is going to be a fabulous way to end the cruise on a happy note."

"Georgie, have no fear! I'm way ahead of you when it comes to cooking up a diversion for tonight. This way!" I followed Gerard into another preparation room in the commissary. I could tell the moment we entered the space that this was the pastry shop. Not just by the sights that assailed us. The air was laden with sweet aromas of coconut, spices, and my favorite—chocolate.

"Behold! A sea of desserts to take their minds off reality and remind them that they came on this cruise for fun and fantasy."

"Oh, my goodness! It's like a scene from that episode of I Love Lucy where Lucy and Ethel are set loose in a candy factory," I exclaimed. Trays and trays of mouth-watering truffles were set out before us on one of the surfaces in this room. A rack was already laden with trays full of them, too.

"Peek in here," Gerard said as he opened the door to a walk-in. Olly-Olly Octopus beamed his wicked smile in a grand display of chocolate. Below him, a smaller, marzipan rendition of Princess Penelope sat among rocky chocolate boulders, her mermaid tail at the edge of a blue-green sugary lagoon. Candy starfish and seashells along with a treasure chest filled to overflowing with gold foil-wrapped chocolate coins surrounded her.

"Now that's a spectacle! The kids are going to go wild."

"Mostly Paolo's handiwork. We were

going to use this at the luau tonight if cruise events had gone as planned. Divine, don't you think?" Gerard sighed, and then went on speaking before I could reply to his question. "The kids can devour Olly-Olly Nemesis of the Deep with impunity. We'll give them little Neptune's Warrior Tridents to use instead of forks. They can dig in and serve themselves while wearing a crown—King Neptune's or Princess Penelope's—as they choose. Hopefully, this will make the evening memorable for other reasons than being stranded at anchor while searching for a man overboard."

As he spoke, Gerard walked me through a wonderland of sweet treats. Staff members, who were busy piping decorations onto cakes of every shape and size, greeted us with friendly nods or hellos as we made our way around the space. Pies and tarts were cooling on racks. Cupcakes and cookies were being iced and turned into fanciful creations.

"All that sugar ought to create quite a buzz. I'm not sure about those pointy tridents, though. I can imagine kids stabbing each other with them once they've had their way with Olly-Olly."

"There's certainly plenty of room to run off that sugar buzz in the kids' areas near where we'll set this up. It's a good idea, though, to have them trade in those tridents for foam rubber toys or blow up pool toys or something like that. I'll make sure the Activities Director has a supply on hand."

"They ought to sleep like babies when that sugar drops them like a rock later," I said. We walked back through the spaces we had traversed to the swinging double doors that led into the storage room. Then to a second set that would return us to a bank of elevators, including the one we had used earlier.

"Let's hope so. Time for the surprise in my cabin. I've got a splendid lunch set up for us. You can invite Jim Rockford if you like."

"Carol's been talking to you, hasn't she?"

"Since I didn't go to the wedding, I had to get the scoop somehow. So, yes, I called your assistant and pumped her for info."

"Jack and I invited you," I said.

"I know. Life at sea is a demanding one. My itinerary is set a year ahead. Now that I've met him, I understand what Carol meant about Jack being a man of action. The way he looks at you, I can believe he was in a hurry to make that walk down the aisle. He does look like James Garner, doesn't he?"

"I think so. Let me call and see if Jack can get away. Bill, too! Be prepared, though. It's going to be your turn to get pumped for information. You have to tell them everything!"

"Tell who everything about what?" Gerard and I both jumped at the sound of the voice that asked that question. Paolo swept in through those swinging doors.

He was no longer wearing that chef's hat and his appearance was even more startling without it. His bright blue eyes were set off by his blond hair that hung straight to his shoulders.

"Gerard has lunch for us. I want him to tell my husband, Jack, all about the spectacles you two have planned for passengers," I lied as fast as my lips could move. It wasn't a complete lie. What I had said was true, just not the whole truth. I'm not sure why I didn't tell him more. *How long had he been down here? How much had he heard already?* I wondered.

6 A DODGY PERROQUET

Stuffed after that lunch with Gerard, Jack seemed quiet but relaxed. I felt wired. When we left Gerard, he was still meeting with Bill Tate going over details after sharing his concerns about the odd things he had noticed in the kitchen and storage areas.

Jack had taken that "fowl play" episode with the duck, as more than play. Less concerned than I had been about scaring the heck out of Gerard, Jack told him to keep his guard up for the duration of the cruise. Gerard agreed and then asked both Bill and Jack what that meant. I don't know about Gerard, but urging him to take precautions had raised my level of anxiety.

"Hearing Gerard's story a second time

gave me the heebie-jeebies," I said once we were alone and on our way to a wraparound promenade on an upper deck. Jack smiled.

"The heebie-jeebies? I haven't heard that term in ages! It's from an old song I can barely remember. Where did that come from?" Jack asked.

"Probably from singing Max's retro-sounding tiki-tiki song with Gerard," I mumbled.

"Singing? Georgie Shaw, what other talents have you been keeping from me?"

It was my turn to smile. With Jack grinning at me, skin-tingling heebie-jeebies weren't all that zipped through me. Snap, crackle, pop, and the anxiety fled. Before I answered him, I grabbed his hands and pulled him close.

"We've only been married one week, Jack Wheeler; surely you don't believe you've learned everything there is to know about me, do you? I'm your mystery woman, remember?" The elevator door slid open behind me. I stepped out, still holding onto one hand, pulling him along with me.

"Well, I am sorry I missed that

performance. When you reveal your singing talents to me, I wouldn't mind if you picked a less annoying song." I laughed feeling more of the tension flee.

"We are a match made in heaven, aren't we? I told Gerard how much I dislike that song. He's already threatened to use that revelation against me."

I explained what I meant by that, as we set out to walk off lunch and the remnants of that bout of the heebie-jeebies. The warm, tropical breeze embraced me. The ship at anchor barely moved in the quiet sea. Blue-green waters shimmered in the afternoon sunshine.

Passengers appeared to be much more at ease than they had been earlier in the day after that announcement about a man overboard. A few hung near the rails watching the vessels patrolling the waters for a missing passenger. Most of the activity was in the family area where parents romped with their kids, splashing noisily in one of the pools, or whooped it up as they slid down a long, curvy water slide. Others lounged in deck chairs, soaking up the sun, reading, or eating and drinking. It would be much quieter when we reached the "adults-only" area of the ship near an elevator we'd take to our cabin.

"Hard to believe anything has gone amiss—until you see that." I pointed to a small craft that had joined the fleet of boats searching the sea around us. A couple of passengers looked up from deck chairs in which they had been reading. Their eyes followed as a cabin cruiser passed by slowly. This one searched at a greater distance from the ship than those that had circled us previously.

"Yes. That mayday went out to all vessels in the area. Volunteers like that guy running his cabin cruiser probably came out here from Raiatea or Bora Bora on his own. I'm always amazed at how willing boaters are to help when someone's in trouble. We see the same thing back in Orange County when there's trouble offshore."

"I guess I should include that in my calculations of the rising scoundrel quotient in our lives. In my life, anyway, since you're probably still way ahead of me when it comes to encounters with bad guys. You do have a way of noticing what's right around you as well as what's wrong, Jack." Jack put an arm around my shoulders, pulling me a little closer.

"Of course, I do. That's how I picked you out of that crowd around a crime scene at Catmmando Mountain on Valentine's Day."

"Lucky for me that you're so perceptive given the evidence was stacking up against me." I slipped my arm through Jack's as we walked along. "What do you think about Paolo as the 'cool blond' who left those hairs on the murdered man? I don't believe it was an accident that he showed up for dessert. I'm sure he was checking up on us—and on Gerard."

"Bill handled that well—keeping the conversation focused on the incidents that Paolo knew about already, and then inviting him to leave before quizzing Gerard about those screams he heard. It would never have occurred to me that the blond was a man. The doc tells me the ones on our victim are phony blond, not natural. I'd never met a blond, blue-eyed Italian before Paolo, but I know they exist despite our stereotypes. Is that hair real or from a bottle of peroxide? I can't tell."

"Gerard seems convinced he's the real deal on many levels. He sings his praises. I hope he'll take our advice that he keep his suspicions to himself and not discuss the investigation with anyone. Maybe I should have emphasized that meant Paolo, too," I offered.

"Gerard seemed suitably impressed about the need to be discrete. Bill had already checked out key staff who have the run of the ship, like Paolo and Gerard. Paolo has an alibi. That doesn't mean he couldn't have had contact with the dead man earlier and left those hairs behind, even if he wasn't the one who stabbed him. Kitchen staff on the early morning shift verified what Gerard told us. Paolo was down in the commissary working on that chocolate octopus you saw. This is off the subject, but that Olly-Olly character is everywhere on this ship. Does the maniacal smile on that thing's face look familiar to you?" I gasped, realizing what he meant.

"A self-portrait by Mad Max! The resemblance is undeniable. Max even arches one eyebrow before he flies into a rage. I dread watching him do that when we meet him in Tahiti. Is there any hope you can identify Passenger X before we catch up with Max even if you don't know who killed Jake Nugent by then?"

"There's nothing new about Passenger X, but they're not letting up on the search. I fingerprinted our dead man and faxed a set of his prints back to my office, along with copies of the identification he had on him. If he has a record and we can flush out known associates, that might help us figure out who killed him. Maybe the man overboard is among that group, and we'll get a photo that someone on board recognizes. That's a long shot. There are a bunch of hoops to jump through to send the body back to the U.S. whether we've figured out who killed him or not. The FBI will do that when they take over the investigation. With a bit of luck, Max can unleash his Rumpelstiltskin tantrum routine on the FBI instead of us."

"What about finding the third man?"

"The cruise ship doctor is no Medical Examiner, but she's pretty sure the assailant is left-handed. I've heard enough reports over the years to believe she's correct. I haven't had a chance to check the video clip Bill sent me to see if the camera caught that."

I sucked in a gulp of air. "Paolo is left-handed, Jack! Maybe he sneaked out of the kitchen and up on deck without anyone in the commissary kitchen seeing him. What if he does peroxide his hair? Can't you get him to give you a sample?" I felt excited at the prospect of having a real suspect

"We could ask him to do that voluntarily, but at this point, there's not enough evidence to demand it. All we know for sure is that Jake Nugent was a passenger who boarded the ship in Tahiti. The identification he had on him matches the information on the Passport found in his room. No one has found a link between him and the crew in the kitchen or elsewhere on the ship at this point."

"At least you can be confident you know who's in the morgue. That's something, anyway. One down, two to go. What about that swatch of material caught on the rail?"

"It's plastic."

"Like a tarp or more like a plastic bag?" I asked.

"Plastic like you'd find in a shopping bag. There's no logo on it so who knows if it's from a shop on board or one visited on shore? Bill has pulled Nugent's shipboard records to see where he's made purchases on board. If we're lucky, that fragment of plastic is from something he bought, and one of the staff in those shops might remember him. More important than that is the possibility that he had a pal or two with him when he made that purchase. It's also possible it has nothing to do with this case. Maybe it wasn't even left there by one of our trio of thieves—if that's what they are." Jack shrugged.

"What do you mean, 'if' that's what they are? Are you changing your mind about the motive behind the murder?"

"We're still operating under the assumption that the killing resulted from a disagreement among thieves. My main aim right now is to preserve evidence until the FBI shows up or we settle on some other chain of custody. That includes the necklace, which, as you suggested, is no prize—it's a cheap piece of costume jewelry. That's one reason I added that 'if' to my statement about these culprits. It doesn't make sense."

"It has to be about the jewelry thefts, Jack. What other reason could Jake Nugent have had for carrying around a copy of a stolen necklace?"

"I suppose Jake Nugent could have grabbed that necklace from the brunette you saw wearing it, believing it was real. He's not much of a jewel thief if he couldn't spot a fake, though."

"If my memory serves me correctly, the necklace she wore looked real although I wouldn't say that about her other assets. Maybe this is about insurance fraud, and she's in on it. Deception apparently doesn't bother her. That could extend to duping her insurance company as well as many of the eligible men on board this ship."

Jack stopped walking and cocked his head to one side. He was amused but feigned mock surprise. "Why, Georgie, that sounds almost catty. If I didn't know better, I'd swear you were jealous of our mystery woman."

"Don't call her a mystery woman. That's me, remember? I'm not jealous. That doesn't mean I'm happy about the fact that this case has you on the hunt for a cool blond and a hot brunette."

"You don't have to worry about me. I am forever immune to the charms of other women, one-week-wife." He put my arm back through his and began walking again. "Nor do I share a history with either of them like you do with the charming Chef Gerard who seems quite taken with you."

"Now who sounds jealous? He's like a brother, Jack. I'm not sure I'm his type if you get my drift."

"Well, I'm not as convinced about that as you are."

"Oh, stop it! Your one-week-wife is mad about you. Isn't that obvious?" We paused, and I used my wifely ways to make him believe me. We could hear squeals coming from somewhere in the distance, but we were alone where we stood wrapped in each other's arms. A ping from my phone broke the spell.

"Max," I said as I looked at the message that went with that ping. "His halo is out. He's delighted to hear we're carrying out, and I quote, 'a thorough investigation with the high degree of discretion necessary to ensure guests have a Marvelous Marley World experience even under such unhappy circumstances.' A halo and hooey! Max is on top of his game, isn't he?"

"Yep, and polishing his media pitch, I see."

"Yeah, some version of it. Let's hope Max holds it together even if this doesn't get wrapped up neatly with a pretty bow on it by the time we meet him in Tahiti."

"Even if Max's horns come out and he has that tantrum that takes him to the center of the earth, I'll be happy to turn this whole mess over to a better-equipped constabulary. They'll have proper investigative facilities and resources at their disposal. In Tahiti, we'll get the evidence we have collected to a lab along with the body. A more formal autopsy could clarify what the killer used as a murder weapon. Our smart and resourceful ship's doctor used her x-ray machine to scan the wounds that killed Nugent. A very sharp-edged blade of some kind. Maybe seven inches in length—longer and not as straight as that boning knife you use all the time. The killer jammed him hard, grazing a rib before piercing his lung. I'm surprised that blade tip didn't break off when it hit the bone. The assailant slashed the artery in his neck too once Nugent hit the ground. That's what killed him."

"That sounds like a fillet knife. Fillet knives are often a little longer than boning knives, with a sharp, pointy, curved blade. Flexible, too, so it could have bent rather than breaking when it nicked that bone. There must be quite a few in the kitchens on this ship. Not that it's still around," I commented as I made a little flicking motion with my hand as though tossing an imaginary knife overboard.

"You're right. It's not likely to be there now. It would have been wise for the killer to throw it overboard as he ran away. Maybe that security video footage caught a glimpse of a knife. I'll check for that, too."

"Gerard and his staff might at least be able to tell you if there's one missing. Was the woman who hollered for the ship's steward able to describe the third man?"

"Not very well. Wendy Cutler's still emphatic that the man who went into the water was pushed overboard by two other men. The steward, David Engels, was at the rail seconds after Wendy Cutler hollered for help. By then, the man was already over the rail and falling so too late to see any pushing and shoving. He could see a second man lying motionless on the deck, and a third man standing near the rails. Engels described the third man as medium height and build, dark hair, partly covered by a hood attached to a dark-colored sweatshirt or baggy jacket of some kind. Rather nondescript like the description the Cutler woman gave us. She claims there was lettering on that shirt—a sports team logo or like the sweatshirts and windbreakers you can buy on board with the Marvelous Marley World corporate logo on them."

"The dead guy was wearing something like that, too, wasn't he?"

"Yes, but she and the steward are confident they were looking at the third man since the second man was already down by then."

"Jewel thieves all dressed alike, imagine that. It sure didn't do much to build team spirit, did it? If they wanted to blend in with other passengers, wearing Marvelous Marley World gear couldn't hurt," I said. "Good camouflage for the killer after fleeing that scene."

"We do have one other bit of information about him. When Wendy Cutler started shouting for help, the third man glanced up at her she says he was wearing glasses. Our dead man wasn't wearing glasses, as you know."

"Unfortunately, I do, having seen Jake Nugent up close. Now I understand why you had Bill Tate take her into protective custody. If

Wendy Cutler saw the killer that means he must have seen her, too."

"Yes, I'm afraid so," Jack sighed. "We're doing all we can to keep her safe until we return to Tahiti. Max better do something nice for her once we get her ashore. Her dream cruise has turned into a nightmare. They've stashed her in the best available unoccupied cabin on the ship. That upgrade's small compensation for what she witnessed this morning and having to finish the cruise in confinement with a security detail on guard around the clock."

"No kidding." I could have said something about our honeymoon not ending as planned, either. Jack was worried, so I restrained myself. Besides, I had no reason to complain. Being married to the man of my dreams, even under the current circumstances, was beyond anything I could have imagined before meeting Jack. I squeezed the arm I held, trying to reassure him.

"A left-handed, dark-haired man wearing glasses with access to a fillet knife. That's progress, Jack. You should get one of the sketch artists on board who does those souvenir portraits for guests to do a drawing based on input from Wendy Cutler and David Engels. That might get you more detail about the third man's appearance. Maybe the second screamer Gerard heard can help, too, if you can find her."

"Georgie, that's a terrific idea about the sketch artist! Bill has to find the second woman Gerard heard screaming before we can ask for her help. Gerard didn't have much to go on, though, and no one else has come forward other than Wendy Cutler. They're going to make another request for help when they update passengers shortly. Not that there's much new to share yet."

"What about the follow up that Bill and Adam did with the passengers involved in that incident report filed about two drunks fighting it out the night before last? Adam said the occupant of the cabin was a woman. If that incident is connected to the mess today, maybe she knows something about what happened." As I paused for Jack to answer, I suddenly heard the pounding of feet behind us. When I turned to look over my shoulder, a large parrot—Perroquet himself—was barreling toward us.

"Good grief! Don't look now, but

Perroquet is heading our way. At least that ridiculous parrot has a French name," I added as I turned back around and pulled Jack with me closer to the rail. That made more room for Perroquet to pass. "Perroquet just means parrot, so not much of a stretch for Max and his Marvelous Marley World 'Marveleers.' With all that marveling, you'd think..."

The sudden impact ended my sentence. It knocked the air out of my lungs and sent me sprawling. I felt like a bird in flight and fought to find my feet. My heart pounded as a second blow seemed to propel me higher and closer to the rail. I kicked out, making contact as I fell. Then, someone grabbed me. Human arms encircled me as I heard someone shout, "Stop!" I struggled and tried to kick again, but it was no use. The memory of that old, futile act to resist on the beach so long ago engulfed me in a wave of dread.

"Not again," I murmured.

7 MIDNIGHT CASANOVA

"Georgie, it's okay! It's me," Jack's lips brushed my ear as he spoke those words. "You're safe. Please don't kick me. Your one-week-husband is no spring chicken. Stop kicking!"

He loosened his grip a little and I spun around, gazed up into his dark brown eyes, and then threw myself against his chest. "Did I hurt you?"

"Not me, but that brute who slammed into us was hobbling when he took off. Good aim! The padding in his costume didn't extend to his knees. I whacked him on the back with a deck chair, and he hardly flinched. That kick you landed when he went for you a second time hurt him."

"A lucky blow, I assure you. My brothers always told me to aim below the belt." After the terror on the beach in Corsario Cove, I had taken a self-defense course and learned to put my brothers' advice into practice. Despite my panic, the instinct to fight had conjured up those old moves. "Serves that feathered freak right. Sorry I didn't get us out of the way in time to avoid a collision."

"That was no accident, Georgie." Jack clutched me in an embrace.

"Word sure got out fast about how much I detest Perroquet. Where's Catmmando Tom when you need him?" Jack held me tighter. He must have sensed how close I was to tears by the quiver in my voice.

"I should never have let you get involved in this trouble," he whispered. A small crowd had gathered, and Jack was trying not to let them overhear us.

"What happened?" a teenaged passenger asked.

"That big parrot ran into her. Then they had a fight," a member of the crowd replied.

"You mean Perroquet?"

"Yeah, that one."

"Is she all right?" someone else asked.

"Aw come on. You know the lady's all right. She's just part of the show," replied the person who claimed to have witnessed the incident. "That guy with her hit Perroquet with a chair and then she kicked that bird. After that, Perroquet took off with these guys chasing him. It was awesome."

"No way! I missed it. Will they do it again?"

"Show's over, folks," Jack said.

"Wow, you were right. It was a show. There must be a new Perroquet movie coming out," the enthusiastic teen said, buzzing with delight.

"They don't look like bad guys, but if Perroquet was trying to stop them, they must have been up to something." There was more discussion as the small group disbursed, but the conversation was lost amid laughter as they departed.

"Are you sure you're okay?" Maggie cried out as she hurried toward us, dodging passengers as the last members of that gathering drifted away. As she approached, I could have sworn I caught a glimpse of Paolo, without his chef's hat, and heading away from us. When I looked more closely, I couldn't see him.

"Better than if I'd gone over the side of the ship from here," I quipped. "I might be in worse shape too if I'd hit the deck when that bird slammed into me. Jack must have grabbed me before that could happen."

"You must not have been so lucky, huh, Jack?" she asked. "Or did you get those from punching that parrot?" Maggie pointed to the knuckles on Jack's right hand that had scrapes on them. "You must have hit your head too," she added. A trickle of blood was slowly making its way down the right side of his face.

"Nothing major. When I tried to catch myself before I hit the ground, I missed the first deck chair and scraped my knuckles. My head, too, I guess. Don't worry, you two. My tetanus shot is up to date." The doctor handed Jack a wipe of some kind, and he swiped at the blood on his face.

"What was it, Jack, if it wasn't an accident?" I asked. I took a second wipe from the doctor and carefully cleaned the knuckles on his hand. Those tears were threatening to appear again. *How close had my one-week-husband and I come to having one of the shortest marriages on record?* I wondered.

"Another Marvelous Marley World character has gone rogue. Most likely intent on delivering a message for us to get out of the way and quit snooping. We must be getting closer to discovering what's going on for someone to take that risk. A man who's already killed two people probably isn't thinking too rationally. A couple of Bill's guys are after him. I doubt he can get far with that bum knee you gave him."

"Being whacked with a deck chair couldn't have felt good either. What an idiotic idea to come after us in that parrot get up. It can't be that easy to move, even uninjured, dressed like that and wearing those big, floppy feet!"

"You'd both better follow me and let me check out that bump on your head, Jack. Just in case. Bill Tate messaged me that he wants us to meet him there, anyway."

"She's right, Jack. Let's go." Jack just nodded as we followed Maggie. When I moved, I got a quick reminder that I was no spring chicken, either. Somewhere in the fracas, I must have twisted awkwardly or worked a few muscles that hadn't been put to the test lately. A sharp pain shot up my leg and into my back. "I could use an aspirin if you don't mind, Doc."

"No problem. It's the least I can do," Maggie replied. Fortunately, we only had a short distance to walk before we arrived at an elevator that could take us below to the infirmary.

As we waited for that elevator, a seabird cried while soaring above us. A gust of air carried a bit of salty spray with it. As the sun moved closer to the horizon, it was taking on that golden hue like the late afternoon sun in California. Normally, that would have been pleasurable. Now it stood in stark contrast to Jack's words. A killer was on the loose and still intent on wreaking havoc, presuming that's who had launched the parrot attack. Time was running out, if it wasn't already too late for Passenger X as Jack's comment about two murders implied.

"Maggie, was that Paolo I saw in the crowd?"

"Yes, it was. When I got the call that there was trouble up on deck, Paolo and I were in the infirmary. He'd dropped by to give us a sample of his hair so we could rule him out as the owner of the strands we've taken into evidence."

"How'd that happen?" Jack asked.

"Bill asked him to do it and he agreed."

"Does that mean he knows about the murder?" I asked.

"I don't think so. Paolo said he wasn't sure why Bill wanted it, but he had nothing to hide and was 'happy to be of service.' Even gave me one of those snappy little bows he does. No peroxide, by the way."

When we arrived at the infirmary minutes later, Bill Tate was there. Maggie brought me a couple of aspirin and a glass of water. Then she checked that scrape on Jack's head before handing him aspirin and water, too.

"Hey, what about me?" In a corner, a half-man-half-bird sat with a dejected look on his face. On the floor, not too far from where he was cuffed to a chair, the top half of his costume gaped at us with huge vacant eyes above an enormous beak. I had a strong urge to start kicking again.

"Meet Justin Michelson, who's in need of some medical attention. He says you took out his knee cap Georgie, as though that was a bad thing." Justin's head snapped up, and he glared at Bill. Jack took a step toward him, and the young man shrank back.

"He's lucky I didn't get to him sooner, or he'd be swimming for it. That's assuming all that padding in his bird suit would have broken his fall when he hit the water from 120 feet up. My wife wouldn't have had that going for her if you'd pushed her overboard as you tried to do, birdbrain."

"No way, Man. That's not what happened. Nobody told me... I mean, I'd never do that." Justin might have had more to say, but Jack took another step toward him, and the squawking stopped.

"How do you like that, Jack? Justin is changing his story already," Bill said. "He told us he grabbed that suit on a whim and was just out for a lark. Running into you was a terrible accident, right, Justin?" Justin didn't make eye contact but nodded. Bill turned to us and spoke before Justin could say a word.

"We got a report a little while ago that a costume last seen in a rehearsal area near the

Sea Nymph stage was missing. No one saw anyone take it, so they figured a stagehand had returned it to the costume room below. When it wasn't there, they reported it stolen."

"Ow! I need some help here. Your wife almost broke my leg, Mister."

"Shut up and sit still, so I don't cut you," Maggie snapped, holding up a pair of scissors. She must have yanked his leg a moment before when she removed the second oversized parrot foot that went with the bottom part of his costume. That left Justin's legs covered in a pair of tights. Rolling a chair close, she began cutting away the material around his knee.

"I was trying to keep you from shoving me overboard, like you did to that man this morning, Justin. It's not Mister, by the way, it's Detective," I said in an indignant tone.

Justin's eyes widened when he heard the word detective tagged on at the end of my accusation about shoving someone off the ship. "Whoa, you can't pin that on me. I was sound asleep when that guy went over the side. I heard somebody pushed him, but it wasn't me, uh, Detective."

"I hope you can prove it. We have a

witness, and you fit her description of the guy who did it pretty well," Jack said in a voice at least as angry as mine. Jack was right! My heart rate sped up as I scanned the young man more carefully.

"Dark hair, dark eyes, a t-shirt rather than a baggy sweatshirt, but Jack, he's even wearing glasses. Justin must be the third man!" I found it hard to believe, looking at the disheveled, belligerent 20-something slouching in his chair.

"Our witness is checking out his passenger photo as we speak. We already have a positive I.D. from the steward who filed that incident report. Meet one of the two men involved in that drunken brawl on Deck 6," Bill commented in a rather offhand manner.

"So, what? That guy tried to stiff me for drinks. That doesn't mean I shoved anyone overboard."

"Well, it does put you near where the trouble occurred this morning. I guess we now know who paid the bar tab. Have you been able to make any connection between him and our dead man in the morgue?"

"Morgue? Dead man? Are you talking

about the guy that went into the water or another one? Ouch! That hurts, Doc!"

"Sorry, but if you keep moving, I can't examine your knee properly." Maggie had cut the tights off both legs and was gingerly checking his knees. "I can take an x-ray to be sure. At this point, I believe our Perroquet impersonator is going to have some ugly bruises, but nothing feels out of place or broken. There's no difference when I compare the two knees, except that the one you kicked is a bit sore and starting to swell." I don't think Justin was paying much attention to her words or I'm sure he would have objected to that "a bit sore" part of her diagnosis. Dead man and morgue still seemed to have his attention.

"What is this? The steward can tell you that the guy with me wasn't dead. We had a few drinks that I charged to my account since Martin didn't have his I.D. with him. More than a few. I'll admit we were pretty wasted. Martin said he had cash in his cabin, but the first cabin he took me to wasn't even his. Then he says he's lost. I thought the loser was jerking me around and told him to stop it or I'd report him to the ship's crew. That's when he took a swing at me. I wrestled him to the ground and was about to help myself to a ring he had in his shirt pocket when that steward broke it up."

"Ring?" I asked. "What kind of a ring?"

"An engagement ring for his girlfriend. The reason he brought her on this cruise was so he could propose. The drinks were to work up his courage to do it."

"At that hour? Did you believe that? What was he—a midnight Casanova?" I blurted that out before I could stop myself.

"I didn't say I believed it. In fact, it sounded like a crock to me. That's why I decided to take the ring—just until he paid me the money he owed me. Before I could do it, that busybody steward butted in and pulled me off him. Yesterday, when I went to the cabin number he gave to the steward, this woman answered. I figured I found his girlfriend, but she acted like she didn't know who Martin Santo was or what the heck I was talking about when I brought up the engagement ring, so I gave up."

"I've only had a chance to glance at the items in the report you gave me about the stolen jewelry, but there was an engagement ring on that list as I recall," Jack commented.

"Yes. One of the first pieces that

disappeared soon after we left Papeete. The woman who reported it missing didn't even call it theft. She thought it slipped off her finger in the spa or pool area and called lost and found. It was only after the other thefts that we added it to the list."

"Stolen jewelry? Dead guys? I need a lawyer, don't I?" Justin asked.

"Unless you want to give up the lame story you told me about going on a spree in that Perroquet costume like a frat boy on spring break. What were you really doing?" Bill asked. Justin looked at Bill then at Jack and back to Bill, avoiding me altogether.

"The lady paid me to do it—the one in the cabin who said she didn't know Martin Santo. She tracked me down today at that bar where Martin and I met. Then she asked me if I knew where he was. I told her I had no clue. That made her cry. Then she showed me that ring. It turns out, they got engaged after all, but she was too upset to tell me about it when I knocked on her door earlier. That's because Martin had ditched her for some other woman—a rich, married one." His eyes bored into me as he spoke. "I woulda' done it for nothing, Jezebel or Georgie or whoever you are."

"Me? Jezebel?" I gasped.

"Yeah. That's what she called you when we watched you walking along, laughing and talking with that man."

"What man?" I asked, incredulous.

"That chef with the high hat," he replied. "Must be lots of men if you can't even figure out who I mean."

"I'm on my honeymoon, Justin!"

"I know that—another reason you suck. I would have done you a huge favor if your wife had gone overboard when I plowed into her." I grabbed Jack's arm as he lunged toward the young idiot. Jack stopped, of course, and in a calm, steady voice said,

"You've been played for a fool, Justin. Your damsel in distress is no victim. Didn't you hear what we just said about that ring being on a list of stolen jewelry?" Justin blinked a couple of times before some of the dots in his head must have suddenly connected to create a different picture. "Here's more for you to consider. If you didn't push that passenger overboard and you didn't kill the guy lying in the morgue, that means there's still a killer running around on this ship. The murderer and his girlfriend are setting you up as a patsy to take the fall for all the trouble on board. Or you're next on the hit list since you got a good look at Martin and his girlfriend."

"I'd listen to Jack. It's no fun being framed or targeted for murder. I'm speaking from experience." Confusion reigned on the young dolt's face. "What was the woman's name?" I asked in a softer tone. I wasn't yet able to feel sorry for him, but I could understand the fear that must be surging through his addled brain.

"Tina," he said. "That's all I know. She didn't give me her last name. She was so upset, I decided to walk back to that cabin with her. The parrot costume was already in there. I didn't steal it from the rehearsal room, she did."

"Lucky for you, if that's true. That costume costs a few thousand dollars—more if it's tricked out with some electronics," I said. "Clearly a felony, right Jack?"

"Oh yes, and that's before you add assault charges. Attempted murder, too, if our friend here meant it when he said you should have gone over the rails."

"That's not what I said. All Tina paid me to do was teach you a lesson about minding your own business and staying away from men who aren't yours. I got into that costume and waited until someone called her and told us where you were. I was having second thoughts, but then she started crying again, so I tore off and did it."

"You have the cabin number Martin Santo gave the steward who broke up the fight. Is the occupant of the cabin named Tina?" I asked Bill.

"Tina Marston," Bill answered after pulling up information about that cabin. "Sounds like we need to have another talk with her. While you patch him up, Maggie, I'm going to get that sketch artist to come down here as soon as Wendy Cutler and David Engels have finished describing the man they saw. Maybe with a drawing based on Justin's description, we can identify Martin Santo and figure out if he's the man overboard, since his name's not on the passenger manifest. I'd hate to believe we have two unidentified passengers on this ship—or did—since at least one of them is swimming with the fishes."

I sucked in a breath of air. There was no humor in that reference to Passenger X in the past tense. Bill must be convinced Passenger X was dead.

"There could be two, though, Bill. Since we still don't know who helped Jake Nugent push Passenger X overboard, why not nominate Martin Santo for that role, too?" I asked.

"Why not? Maybe this ship is crawling with stowaways!" Bill responded. "I admit, it's hard to believe Justin's the third man. Just in case, I'll find out what Wendy Cutler and David Engels say about it after checking out Justin's passenger photo." I had to agree that Justin hardly fit the part of a skilled slasher. As he reached out for the aspirin Maggie offered him, I knew for sure.

"Not our slasher," I muttered as Justin reached for it with his right hand. Jack heard me and nodded in agreement. My spirits took a nosedive for a moment, forcing me to realize how disappointed I was that the wretch in that Perroquet costume had not been the ruthless "third man." Was it Martin Santo? Was he the one who had called Tina and given her the signal to turn Justin loose in that stupid outfit?

Did Tina Marston know who he was and how to find him?

8 PATTY, PATSY—WHATEVER

Jack and I waited for Bill to round up Tina. When they got to her cabin, minutes later, there was no sign of her. Surprise, surprise! She must have been intelligent enough to realize any guy willing to fall for her jilted female routine wasn't too bright. I doubt she had counted on his ability to elude shipboard authorities, even if he'd been able to use the escape route she suggested. Hobbling, and with security on his heels, he hadn't removed that stolen costume and ditched it overboard as she had instructed him to do.

There was also no indication that Martin Santo or any other man had been in Tina's cabin. Her getaway was much more successful than Perroquet's. She had cleared out her stateroom and then invited housekeeping to clean it. The only good news, apart from the fact that I was still shipboard, was that the sharp-eyed doctor had spotted another of those blond hairs. Not in Tina's cabin but elsewhere.

She found this one stuck to a Velcro flap exposed as Justin sat there wearing only the bottom half of that costume. A quick comparison with the two collected earlier from Jake Nugent's body led Maggie to conclude it was probably a match.

"Without better equipment, it's impossible to be sure," Maggie had cautioned us. Still, I felt buoyed by the prospect that we had found another tangible link to a person involved in more than one of the incidents that had occurred today. That, along with Justin's claim that he had seen Tina in possession of the stolen engagement ring, also tied the events to the jewelry thefts.

"Was the woman who paid you to run her errand a blond?" Jack asked Justin after Maggie found that hair. The photo Bill had obtained from Tina's profile portrayed her as an attractive brunette.

"Nah, Tina's a brunette, with a cute smile and a great body from working out. That

Martin Santo's a crazy man to ditch her. I guess he thought he was going to get a woman with money..."

"Are you going back to that again?" Jack asked.

"A box of rocks," Maggie murmured under her breath.

As in "dumber than," I presumed without asking. "Any reason we can't turn Justin around to face the wall while we make him sit in the corner?" I asked.

"What difference is it going to make to a box of rocks?" Maggie retorted.

"Is this Tina?" Bill asked, pulling up a picture on his phone of the woman from the passenger roster named Tina Marston.

Justin had been slouching in his seat again. When he saw that picture, he became excited and tried to stand. "Yeah, that's her!" A reaction followed that he surely should have anticipated.

"Ow, ow, ow!" He shouted as his bum knee protested and the cuffs on one arm yanked him back like a dog that had gone too far on its chain. When the rebound slung him back into his seat, awkwardly, he yelped again.

"Noisy for a box of rocks," Bill said as the screen on his cell phone went dark. "If it's all right with you, Maggie, I'm going to move him out of here and into the brig."

"No problem. I'll wrap that knee for Justin. I'll check on him again later after he's had dinner."

Who knew? A brig and a morgue on a luxurious cruise liner, I thought.

"That's assuming he can eat given how much pain he's in," Jack added with a smirk on his face.

"I can eat," Justin retorted. "Not that I like being locked up in a cage like uh, uh..." He shut up after looking at the remnants of the big, padded, feathered parrot suit he was still wearing.

"Can you get our jailbird a change of clothes, Bill?" Jack asked.

"Sure. You might find this interesting, Jack. It was in a drawer in his cabin." Bill handed Jack a clear plastic bag that contained a sweatshirt with the Marvelous Marley World logo and slogan on it:

"It's a marvelous world...a Marvelous Marley World!" The dark color certainly fit the description of the one given by the eyewitnesses who had caught a glimpse of the slasher on Deck 6. "Wendy Cutler said there was some kind of writing on the shirt the third man was wearing this morning before he took off, but still says she can't be certain what it said. I showed her pictures of Justin. She doesn't think he's the man she saw running away after killing Jake Nugent, but she wants to take a closer look at him, in person."

"Hey, wait a second. I already told you I was sleeping this morning when that Oscar alarm went off. That's not my shirt, either! I have one, but it's got Catmmando Tom on it. Can you bring me that one and a pair of sweatpants so I can get out of this parrot outfit?"

"Please," I added. Justin shot daggers at me before speaking.

"Please," he said, shaking his head in disgust.

"I suppose you're going to tell me this isn't yours, either, even though we found it in your cabin." Bill held up what appeared to me to be a diamond tennis bracelet. It was in another plastic bag, much smaller than the first one holding that sweatshirt. "Another item originally reported to lost and found and now on the list of stolen jewelry," Bill said as he handed that bag to Jack.

"Those are real diamonds, Jack." I peered at the bracelet as he turned that bag over and then flattened the bag out on the palm of his hand. "White gold, too. Not high end, but not cheap costume jewelry like that necklace Jake Nugent had on him."

"My wife has a good eye for shiny things," Jack said, winking. Despite that wink, I could tell he was worn out. Justin had his mouth open, ready to squawk again. I jumped back in with a question before the young fool could speak. I toyed with the idea of mentioning that Justin was right-handed unlike our slasher, but why take the weasel off the hook. Besides, even if he wasn't the killer that didn't mean he didn't have some other connection to the thievery ring that he hadn't revealed. Maybe he wasn't the box of rocks he pretended to be.

"Do you know where the owner lost it?"

"In the lounge area near the women's spa and fitness center. And, yes, before you ask, that's one of the areas where other passengers told us jewelry went missing, including that engagement ring," Bill added.

"The cool blond hanging out with the thieves must like shiny things as much as Klepto-Kitty and I do, Jack." Bill, Justin, and Maggie stared at me. I didn't have time to explain about Klepto-Kitty before Justin bellowed.

"I'm no klepto-anything. I've never seen that bracelet before, and I told you Martin Santo had the ring that's missing, not me. Somebody's trying to make me a patty. You said it yourself!"

"Derek!" Bill bellowed suddenly. The door to the infirmary opened, and a young man darted into the room.

"Yes, Sir. What is it?"

"Go back to that cabin we were searching and bring a sweatshirt—any one you can find quickly—and sweatpants, please."

"Right away," Derek said as he left the room.

"Georgie has a point. The elusive blond certainly has some association with the trouble on this ship since she's now popped up twice—her hair has anyway," Jack commented.

"She would have had access to those locations that are restricted to women only. Maybe the three men fighting it out on Deck 6 this morning had some help from the woman whose hair we found on the late, Jake Nugent."

"That makes sense, Georgie. If Tina's not hiding out somewhere with Martin Santo, she could be doubling up with the blond. I don't suppose there's an easy way to screen passengers for hair color, is there, Bill?"

"Why not ask the Spa Attendants," I said. "A cool blond might stand out if she's been a regular down there. Justin mentioned that Tina works out. If they know each other, they could have shown up together. You have a picture of Tina to show them. Guests leave cabin numbers when they make appointments. Maybe Tina's cabin number and the one that belongs to our unknown blond will turn up on the same day if the know each other. And, and on days that passengers reported they lost jewelry. We'll start by asking about the women, showing them that picture of Tina. Then we'll ask them to search for the days when Tina's cabin number appears. After that..." When I looked up, the others were staring at me.

"What? Am I repeating myself? You're not still waiting for an explanation about Klepto-Kitty, are you?" I asked.

"I don't know about the others," Bill responded. "I was wondering how you could be thinking as clearly as you are after all that's gone on today. Especially after that whooping you gave to the parrot who now realizes he's a patsy." Bill turned toward Justin before adding, "It's a patsy, Justin, not a patty." Justin shrugged.

"Patty, patsy—whatever," he said.

"Once we get Justin situated in the brig, I'll see if I can find someone to follow up on your suggestions about questioning the Spa Attendants. We're stretched to the limit as you can imagine."

"All-hands-on-deck, I'm sure," I said sympathetically. He was right that I was tired and stressed out, but until today, I'd been living it up. Bill and the rest of the crew had been working round-the-clock for the past week at sea before the trouble today. He had to be exhausted.

"You've got it. Everybody's on notice

that we're all on extra duty until we're back in Papeete. It's not my crew members out on the water searching for Passenger X, but we have Security Associates guarding our eyewitnesses, Wendy Cutler and David Engels, the morgue, and we'll have to keep watch on Justin in the brig. We've stepped up patrols throughout the ship, too, with that slasher still on the loose." At the mention of his name, followed shortly after that by a reference to a "slasher," Justin squirmed. I sure hoped, for his sake and ours, that he wasn't holding out on us.

"I've got guys reviewing all the footage collected over the past week anywhere on Deck 6. They're searching for any sightings of our dead man, Jake Nugent, or our woman on the run, Tina Marston. They have a sketch of the third man involved in that brawl this morning, so if they spot anyone that looks like him in that area, they'll let me know. Adam is running down information from Sales Associates in the shops where Nugent made purchases, and I'm going to have him do the same for Tina Marston. I'll make sure that he asks about a blond with shoulder length hair in case she was with Marston while she was shopping. Max Marley doesn't skimp on the staff-to-guest ratio on board, but we are maxed out."

"I don't mind dropping by and asking a few questions at the spa if you're all right with that. Jack and I do need to clean up and change for dinner. What do you think, Jack?"

"You're unstoppable, Georgie," Jack said. "Can you email us a copy of that photo of Tina Marston, Bill? We'll visit the spa on our way to dinner even if it means we'll be a little late. We've promised to drop by that Olly-Olly Free, Free, Free Desserts of the Deep extravaganza, first, though."

"Jack's a devotee of that 'eat-dessert-first' edict, Bill. We don't dare miss it. Not that a chocoholic like me would let that happen. It might mean we'll be a little late for our dinner reservation at The Captain's Table."

"Don't worry about that. The Captain won't be offended. He's not going to appear at tonight's seating. The bridge is busy staying in communication with everyone involved in the search for our man overboard. They intend to use every minute they have left before we have to get underway in the morning."

"We'll give you a call later, after we've made our visit to the spa—if we learn anything useful," Jack said as we left the infirmary.

"Sure thing," Bill said. As we were leaving, a man with a goatee entered with a sketch pad tucked under one arm.

Good casting, I thought. Was that his idea or another of Max's hiring criteria? I could see Max sitting behind his desk with the fingers on both hands touching, creating the little pyramid mastermind gesture he often adopted while brainstorming. I could hear his pronouncement: "Goatee required to play the role of shipboard sketch artist." I only wished he were sitting behind that desk, now, instead of flying to meet us in Tahiti.

"Let's get a move on," I said picking up my pace.

"That ol' devil Max on your heels," Jack asked.

"How did you know?"

"You straightened your shoulders and put your chin up the way you do when you head off to work. Besides, Ari'i nui as Bill calls him— is on my mind, too. Come on, I'll race you." Jack took off with a burst of speed.

"And you call me unstoppable! Give me a break, please? I'm a victim of one of Max's deranged surrogates. I can't run! Don't leave me alone like this!" He stopped, dashed back my way, and swept me into his arms.

"How could I ever leave a classy dame like you alone? You've got your hooks into me—deep, Sweetheart." he said playing the role of fake film noir detective again. There was nothing fake about the kiss that followed, however. That put a little oomph in my step as we returned to our suite.

When Jack and I returned to our suite to shower and dress for dinner, it was clear my clothes had taken a beating in the wrestling match with Perroquet. At some point in the melee, I had torn my knit shirt and had lost a button on my black pants. My Espadrilles were more than a little scuffed. Jack's one-week-husband anniversary clothes weren't in great shape either.

"Maybe I should assume crime-fighting is just what we do to bond as a couple, Jack, and pack appropriately from now on. Where'd you get those police tactical pants? Do they take a credit card? How about red—do they come in red, my one-week-husband?"

Jack, who was in our bathroom taking his second shower of the day, didn't reply. "I don't think he can hear me," I said to the cats.

They had greeted us warmly at the door, but both were now on alert. I had tossed my clothes into a corner when I slipped into my robe. I was now adding Jack's trashed aloha shirt and torn shorts to that heap. The cats jumped as I tossed each item on that pile, and then went back to warily inspecting the damaged goods.

"You two know when Mom and Dad have been up to no good don't you?" Miles bellowed in reply. "I wonder where my husband's snazzy new Panama hat has gone." I couldn't even remember the last time I'd seen it on Jack's head.

The bed in our room looked incredibly comfortable. I was tempted to drop back into it. Who knows what remnants of a day at sea wrestling desperados had left on my body? I flashed on Jake Nugent, lying in that pool of his own blood.

"Eew," I thought, *"a shower it is."*

"Your turn, Doll," Jack said, slipping up behind me. I jumped at the sound of his voice. When I did that, both cats sprang about a foot off the floor and took off. Jack and I laughed at the sight.

"Guilty conscience, Jezebel?" he asked

looking every bit the man on a luxury cruise in his MMW Fantasy of the Sea robe.

"You left the shower running, and I didn't hear you coming. Sneaking up on me is not a bit funny after the day I've had. I'm now adding stealth to my one-week-husband's list of hidden talents, a dubious distinction I might add."

"In my defense, I wasn't trying to be stealthy. Forgive me, please? Cross that hidden talent off my list and put poet on it, instead. Remember that verse I penned for you this morning in celebration of our one week anniversary?" When I didn't answer immediately, he pulled me into his arms. His hair, still damp from that shower, smelled clean with a hint of sandalwood and coconut in the mix. I let him kiss me about twenty times before I relented.

"Okay, okay, I forgive you. I'm going to shower and hope the hot water soothes my aches and pains."

"I've got a better suggestion than that. The water is running in there for you, and I dropped one of those fizzy bath bomb things you like into the tub. I have material to review, this report to put together, and I need to touch base with Adam and Bill about a couple of things. I'm getting dressed. You have a soak in the tub and pretend you're on your honeymoon."

"Are you sure? That does sound heavenly—even all by myself." I smiled coyly.

"You may not be Jezebel but you are a temptress, my love. Duty calls, though. The sooner this mess is over, the sooner we can get back to what really matters. Ari'i nui is on his way, after all."

"You'd better try to get those cats to forgive you before you get dressed. They're not pushovers like me. They're going to want to hear a full-fledged apology complete with treats." When I said that magic word, the duo reappeared in the doorway to our room. Miles tilted his head back and bellowed. Ella chattered, backing him up.

"Treats!" Jack said, loudly, this time. "You aren't mad at me, are you?" I heard him ask his two companions as they led him out of our bedroom. Their tails stood straight up.

"Speaks cat fluently," I said aloud as I stepped into the tub, adding to my one-week-husband's lists of talents. "Likes to buy me shiny things, too," I added as I caught site of the gorgeous floral sheath I planned to wear to dinner. The neckline would be perfect for my one-week anniversary gift.

9 SPAS AND GOSSIPS

On our way to the Olly-Olly dessert extravaganza, Jack and I did as we had promised and dropped by that spa. The moment we walked into Penelope's Spa & Fitness Retreat I felt myself relax. Great care had been taken to create a peaceful ambiance. Soft music played with a slow rhythmic beat—not too different from that of a pulsing heart at rest.

Clever, I thought as I felt my breathing slow to match that beat. It worked its magic on Jack, too, even though he's no fan of places that sell expensive "gunk and goop," as he calls it. I could feel the tension flee from him as he breathed in the aromatic balm of lavender spiked with hints of Tahitian vanilla. Just like the scent in that luxurious bath I had taken in our suite. That had been so relaxing, in fact, I had dozed off. I felt ready to go another round or two.

The information desk sat in an alcove surrounded by a moving picture wall like the one in our suite. This one contained breathtaking video images of a flowing waterfall surrounded by gorgeous tropical flowers in full bloom.

"Can I help you?" a young woman asked. Kayla, as her name tag read, was dressed in a Sarong and wore an orchid tucked behind one ear. Her smile was as pleasant as the surroundings in which we stood.

"We hope so," I responded in a quiet voice. "There's been some trouble on board today, as you know. I work for Marvelous Marley World management," I said as I slid my I.D. card across the counter. "We're trying to locate two women we hope might have information about the passenger who went overboard this morning."

"Pushed overboard, you mean," Kayla said as wariness washed that warm smile from her face. She picked up my I.D. card and glanced at it. Without saying a word, her eyes wandered to Jack. He had reacted ever so slightly to her reference to the passenger as having been pushed. I don't think she noticed his reaction but wondered who he was. That's how Jack read it, too.

"I'm Detective Jack Wheeler, Kayla. Marvelous Marley World has asked me to help sort out what happened to the passenger this morning. Who told you that passenger was pushed overboard?" Jack flashed his badge. I hadn't realized he'd brought that with him on this trip until I saw it lying on the bar next to our room key and his cell phone this morning. My boy scout is always prepared. I'll give him credit for that.

"It's been part of the buzz in here all day. The main topic of discussion, in fact, until Perroquet went wild and mowed down a couple of older passengers a little while ago. They're probably out of commission for the rest of the trip. What a jerk," she added quickly. "You know about that already, don't you?" Wariness turned to outright suspicion as she asked that question.

"Yes, of course. The culprit's in custody. We're also aware of rumors that someone pushed the missing passenger overboard," I said. "Do you have any idea how those rumors got started?"

"Sure," Kayla responded, although she appeared more puzzled than sure about anything. "Some woman was screaming about it at the top of her lungs, that's how. Our first client of the day came in for a massage, irate about the fact that the woman had nearly knocked her down as she ran past her on the upper deck. She was yelling that she saw two men shove a passenger over the rails and into the water."

"Did your client see her ask a staff member or anyone else for help?"

"No. Part of the reason our guest was so ticked off is that she had tried to get her to do that. She asked the woman something like, 'did you tell security?' The woman cussed her out and screamed at her. 'Are you crazy? I don't want to be next!' To which our client replied 'Oh, I get it. That's why you're so hush-hush about it.' The woman shut up at that point and ran for it."

"Can you give us the name of that guest who encountered the distraught woman, please?" Jack asked. "Maybe she can help us identify the woman she spoke to this morning.

Security has probably already tracked her down, but we want to be certain we've contacted everyone who has any information about what went on."

Kayla nodded, her fingers clicking away on the keyboard in front of her. She glanced at the computer screen and then wrote a name and cabin number on one of the appointment cards they give out to guests. Smiling, Kayla handed that card to Jack. "Hope this helps you find what you're looking for," she added with a smile.

"Thanks," I replied, getting her to let go of that card she had offered to Jack. "That brings me back to why we're here. Have you seen this woman?" I showed her a photo of Tina Marston.

"Oh yes, that's Tina Marston," she responded. "We call her 'Monster Marston' around here because of the monstrous workouts she does. She's the one who gave us that nickname she earned during her military service."

"Can you check to see if she was in here for appointments on Monday, Tuesday, or Thursday?" I asked.

"I don't have to check those dates. Tina scheduled a massage every day. Her routine was pretty much the same—a killer workout first thing in the morning, followed by taking the waters, and then a massage. She was here for a couple hours at least. Never missed a workout. Never late for an appointment. The perfect client," Kayla added.

"Taking the waters?" Jack asked.

"It's a series of baths, Jack—really quite rejuvenating," I responded, with a bit too much enthusiasm for someone there on business. I'd indulged myself this week and my mind drifted back to that blissful bath I'd just taken. Soaking in warm, soothing scented balms seemed so much better than asking questions about women who might be involved in a theft ring and murder. I tried to switch back to a more professional tone. "You really should try them out for yourself, Detective. They have the same service for men." Too late.

"I knew I'd seen you before," Kayla said. "You were leaving the spa yesterday just as I started my shift. I heard this was a honeymoon cruise for you." Suspicion stole over her as she looked at me, glanced at Jack, and then fixed her gaze on me. I almost blushed, waiting for her to cry, "Jezebel" as Justin had done earlier.

A sideways glance at Jack must have revealed some clue to the fact that my embarrassment was morphing into indignation. He fought to keep a smile on his lips from spreading across his face. Then, before I could say another word, he changed the subject speaking in a friendly, matter of fact tone.

"You've been very helpful to our investigation, Kayla. Just one more question before we go." He beamed a Jim Rockford smile at her that worked like a charm. Suspicion fled, along with any regard for my presence at all as far as I could tell.

"Have you noticed a woman with shoulder-length, blond hair in here this week? Perhaps working out with Tina or in here around the same time?"

"Oh sure. You're talking about Abby Kinkaid. She's in good shape, but no way could she keep up with Monster Marston. An odd friendship, but that's one of the interesting outcomes of being on a cruise—you meet all sorts of new people. Abby was almost as disciplined about her fitness routine as Tina. Not today. Neither of them showed up—not even Tina—so even she's not the perfect client, is she?" She shrugged.

"I guess everyone's knocked off balance by the sad events this morning and the change in our itinerary," I said. It occurred to me, though, that neither woman had an alibi for what went on this morning. If Abby had been with Jake Nugent before he became embroiled in a fight to the death on Deck 6, that would explain how he picked up those blond hairs.

"Yeah, guests are upset about the idea of some guy floating around out there, lost or drowned. It's been surprisingly good for business here, though. Until that dessert pig-out started a little while ago, passengers were lined up in here." She lowered her voice as she spoke those last words as another Spa Attendant passed us with a client at her side. "It's slowed down a lot, but we still have more bookings than we would have had if we'd made it to Bora Bora and guests had gone ashore today."

"How about a cabin number for Abby Kinkaid and then we'll let you get back to work, all right?" Jack said with another of those dazzling smiles on his face. Kayla hopped to it and typed the Kinkaid woman's name on the keyboard, a loopy grin on her face.

I added a drooling redhead to the sultry brunette and cool blond on the list of women of interest to this investigation. Inwardly, I harrumphed, wondering if it would be fair to ask my one-week-husband to rely less on his masculine charm in his police work. I snapped back into snoop mode and asked one last question of my own.

"Do Abby and Tina use the same lockers when they're in here or do you assign them new ones each time?"

"Since they're regulars, they have the same lockers for the duration of the cruise."

"I'm afraid I just lied to you, Kayla," Jack said. "We're going to need to look at those lockers before we leave."

"Jack, I don't believe Kayla's going to want you roaming around in the women's locker room. Why don't I call Maggie and ask her to join me as soon as she can get up here?" Jack nodded and then sighed.

It was my turn to read his thoughts. "Eat dessert first," was written on that sigh. I wanted to reach out with a reassuring touch, but that might earn me another of those 'shameless hussy' glances from the auburn-haired Spa Attendant. For the moment, Kayla had no interest in me at all. She was intent on answering an unrelated question Jack had asked her about "taking the waters." A perfect distraction while I tracked down Maggie and spoke to her.

"Maggie," I said as soon as she answered my call. "It's Georgie. Can you come up to the spa for a few minutes—bring your gloves and baggies and those tweezers you use to pick up hairs. If we're lucky, we may have a few more for you."

Twenty minutes later Maggie and I had completed the task. Maggie bagged everything left in both women's lockers: a sweatband and an ointment for pain relief in Tina's locker along with a bathing suit and a small bag of toiletries. We found similar items in Abby's space, along with an extra change of clothes. Nothing struck me as unusual about anything we found. The effort had proved useful in another way, however. Not only had we located several more strands of blond hair from Abby's locker, but we discovered a dark brown hair, too. Monster Marston's cubbyhole had also yielded a couple of hairs—dark ones. The question I hoped Maggie could answer was would those blond hairs from Abby match those she had collected already? Had we discovered the identity of our cool blond?

On our way to that dessert fest, Jack and I discussed what we had learned from our visit. As it turned out, Jack's casual conversation with Kayla had been very revealing. When Jack ventured onto the subject of spa treatments for men—like taking the waters—he mentioned Jake Nugent. Like Abby and Tina, Jake Nugent had also been a regular guest at the spa and fitness center. Several expensive watches and a signet ring on that list of missing jewelry had gone missing on dates Jake Nugent had visited the spa or fitness center.

"What a busy little circle of thieves. Smart, too, that no one caught them in the act. Have you found out more about who Jake Nugent is—or was before that third man murdered him this morning?"

"Yes. That's only one of the things I worked on while you were snoozing in the tub. He's a regional sales rep for a jewelry company in Dallas."

"Wow! That means he knew a thing or two about jewelry."

"Very true. Jake Nugent traveled throughout the Southwest visiting the company's retail outlets with the newest designs, new inventory, and company sponsored sales on older items. The background report is rather general, but he had been with the same company for ten years. He made good money but seemed to have had plenty of expenses, too, including alimony to an ex-wife."

"From what you've told me before, Jack, money problems might explain how a man with a steady job in the jewelry business could get mixed up with thieves."

"Also, true, Georgie. Money is second only to love as a motive for murder and mayhem."

Before he could say more, our conversation ended abruptly.

10 EAT DESSERT TWICE

"Welcome, Georgie! You look gorgeous. That's beautiful, too," he said examining my pendant. "Welcome, Jack! I'm so glad you could make it. Paolo's display is a huge success. Olly-Olly is taking some hits, as you can see." My old friend had been on the lookout when we arrived at the entrance to the dessert extravaganza. He had swept us into the banquet room, decked out for the event with colorful streamers, balloons, and other decorations.

I followed Gerard's pointing finger and watched as children stood in line to stab at Olly-Olly's tentacle set on a table low enough for children to reach without help from adults. It was an impressive display, with those chocolate arms winding their way down two sides so kids could go at it from either side. A parent held up a child who took aim higher up at Penelope's nemesis.

"Take that, Olly-Olly," the child cried as a hunk of chocolate landed on her plate. Several other kids followed suit, uttering that cry or a similar one, and the clash of tridents was on!

Given that hundreds of passengers roamed about the space in which Gerard had set out his fantasyland of desserts, it was remarkably well-ordered chaos. Two dozen separate stations were set up around the perimeter of the large space. Kitchen staff darted expertly around the buffet lines, replacing empty platters with new ones, straightening up off-kilter serving dishes, and tidying the buffet tables as they went.

Servers waited on seated passengers as well, bringing beverages and other items to their tables. Champagne corks popped as servers poured out the bubbly to adults in attendance. I could smell the heavenly aroma of coffee. Servers whizzed by with coffee pots and pitchers of milk. Along with the sugar buzz from chatty passengers, dishes clanked as they were placed on tables or whisked away.

"I smell peanut butter," Jack announced suddenly. "I was hoping you'd have macadamia nut pie, but peanut butter cookies will do."

"There's no shortage of nuts, macadamia or otherwise, I assure you. Plenty of chocolate, too, for even a discriminating chocoholic like you, Georgie. Follow me, you two. I have a table set up for us in an out of the way corner. We'll dig in along the way. I'll happily serve as your guide to all the delights on Penelope's reef of treasures and treats."

As Gerard moved, it was as if the seas parted. Perhaps, it was his tall hat that towered above most everyone in the room. He snapped his fingers and kitchen staff were upon us with china plates and utensils. Jack and I followed as Gerard rattled off the names of items that lined Penelope's "reef," a display comprised of faux rocks and coral shelves repeated in many locations around the room. Other passengers leaned in, listening to the Chef's descriptions of the mouth-watering desserts.

When we reached our seats, Jack and I each had two plates. One of my plates contained nothing but chocolate truffles with a variety of fillings. The other held a small square of coconut pineapple cake adorned with a golden spiral of spun sugar, and a sliver of that macadamia nut pie Jack had hoped to find. When I sat down, I attacked the cup of coffee before me, and then tackled those truffles. The effect was immediate. My energy and mood surged.

"Bravo, Gerard. These are excellent. Even though I've seen your workspace with my own eyes, I'm stunned that you could pull this off," I said.

"Paolo's not the only chocolatier aboard. That's what made me decide we'd sweeten things up tonight with a dessert bonanza. Since Paolo's centerpiece was going to be part of our luau celebration if we'd kept to our original plan to party on the beach in Bora Bora tonight, we had a head start on that piece. Our other pâtissier was away from her station when you were in the commissary, or I would have introduced you to her. She went into high gear when I told her what we had in mind for tonight and helped produce mass quantities of truffles to die for!"

Inwardly, I winced at that "to die for" phrase. "To chocolatiers!" I said, raising my cup of coffee in a toast. "Please thank her for us." Jack nodded as he continued to pack away the desserts on his plate, his mouth too full to say a word. I drained that cup of coffee and poured more. I still had plenty of chocolate and sugar left in front of me when Jack's phone rang. Although he had done a much better job than me of devouring his desserts, he wasn't quite finished yet, either.

"Excuse me," Jack said as he stepped away from our table to take that call. I continued to chat and give Gerard feedback about those truffles—mostly "mm's" and "ah's." I tried to be pleasant and make conversation even though I was anxious about that call.

When he returned, Jack was not wearing the happy face that truffles, a peanut butter brownie bite, a triple salted-caramel mini-cupcake, and macadamia nut pie with vanilla ice cream had put there before he answered his phone. Our dalliance over dessert was at an end.

"I'm sorry, Gerard, to eat and run, but duty calls. If I've ever had better desserts, I don't know when or where—except for the ones my wife whips up, of course," Jack added a wink that was supposed to reassure me. It did not. I could tell he was upset.

Gerard smiled, but a worried expression

warred with that smile. He knew something was up, too. When we sat down, I had used Jack's "eat dessert first" adage to explain why we were having dessert before dinner. I had not mentioned that we might also have to leave in haste. Still, Gerard got it.

"No need to apologize. I understand that the reasons you have to 'eat dessert first' don't always allow you to explain when it's time to go." In a quieter voice, Gerard added. "Please be careful. It sounds like you two were already warned once today about getting into the middle of whatever's going on." I tried to hide my surprise.

"How did you hear about that?" I asked.

"Bill Tate mentioned it when he dropped by to discuss security precautions in place for this event. Maybe your dislike of Penelope and Perroquet's song was a premonition, Georgie," Gerard replied.

That Bill had been the source of information about our mishap was a relief. "I won't say it was a premonition, but it has done nothing to improve my attitude about that song," I said. "We'll be careful, Chef. I hope you're doing everything by the book as Bill has asked you to do."

"As if it's a recipe for staying alive and well, Georgie." He stood and snapped his fingers again. When a member of the kitchen staff rushed to respond, Gerard said only a few words: "Take-outs, please!"

The young woman in kitchen whites tore off and was back in a flash with take-out boxes bound by elastic ribbon and topped with silvery bows and a fresh orchid. "Just in case you were unable to join us, I put together some treats for you. Eat dessert twice has to be about as good as eating dessert first, don't you agree?"

"Aw, how lovely. Thanks, Gerard," I said giving my old friend a hug. The thoughtfulness of that gift had raised Jack's spirits too.

"Why not 'eat dessert twice?' Especially if it involves chocolate, right Georgie?'

"If you can get away with it..." I was about to add something about how many hours of gym time Jack and I ought to log in the wake of our over-indulgence. Before I could finish that sentence, however, Paolo appeared as if he had just materialized out of thin air.

"Get away with what?" Paolo asked. A blinding smile radiated as he moved around from behind Gerard and stepped close to me.

His piercing blue eyes glittered as he waited for my response.

"Eating dessert twice," I replied, as I stood to leave. Jack took a step toward the exit. Paolo glanced his way and promptly directed his gaze back to me.

"No! Please don't tell me you are leaving so soon." Paolo reached out and took my hand. Then as if in a scene from one of those period pieces of the cinema featuring the European aristocracy or continental Romeos, he kissed it! I pulled my hand back and stood there in disbelief. Before speaking again, Paolo raised one hand in an operatic gesture as Pavarotti might do.

"I was hoping to hear you enjoyed the chocolate that Gerard says makes you smile. A smile I have already seen that is as bright as the sun at dawn even without my inspired chocolate."

I heard a small cough come from Jack. Or maybe it was the sound he makes when he clears his throat before speaking. We were in a hurry so that could explain the noises. Still, I couldn't help but notice that Jack had clenched his jaw in a tense, angry way.

That ticked me off. Surely, Jack couldn't believe Paolo's flattery worked on me? If anything, it had almost the opposite effect. I'd fought the urge to slap his face for his cheekiness. I'm no sucker for smooth talkers, even pretty ones, like Paolo. Nor did I miss the fact that his high opinion of my smile was most likely a pale second to his regard for his inspired chocolate. In any case, it was time to go. Jack spoke before I could say goodbye.

"Sorry, Pal. You're out of luck. Georgie's had all the sugar she can handle for one night. We're in a rush, so we'll have to discuss your inspired chocolate another time. Thanks again, Gerard. Ciao, Paolo!" Jack reached out and cupped my elbow with his hand, ushering me toward the door. I waved as we made our way through the crowd and out the door onto the deck of the ship. I caught a smile and a little bow in return from Paolo before he slipped into the seat Jack had occupied.

Maybe I was no fool for Paolo, but Gerard beamed as Paolo sat down facing him. I'm not sure why I felt so uneasy about Gerard's fascination with Paolo. I hoped he was keeping quiet about the investigation on board and taking precautions as Bill had advised him to do—even with Paolo.

"Sorry, Georgie. That was more than rude. Are you mad at me?"

"A little if you consider me the sort of woman who would fall for any of that baloney. I recognize fake charm when I see it."

"It's not that. I just couldn't stand the way the guy was ogling you—and with me standing right there. He's like a male version of Jennifer's tacky friend, Caroline Chambers."

I paused for a moment recalling how annoyed I had become when she fawned over Jack the night we met her at a restaurant in Corsario Cove.

"I know what you mean. Caroline was working it that night. She had an excuse, at least, since we weren't even officially a couple at the time. It's that blond, blue-eyed Romeo-wannabe who was rude." I shuddered a little. "There's something about him that makes me want to go wash that hand he just kissed. Why can't Gerard see that, Jack?"

Jack tucked my arm around his and moved us along. "Gerard hasn't been as fortunate as we have been to find true love and trustworthy friends, I guess."

"Maybe he needs our help. I know Paolo

has an alibi, and I'm sure the cruise line checked him out before they hired him, but don't you have someone who can snoop and see if he's got a criminal history of some kind?"

"Not officially." Jack stopped speaking for a moment, perhaps considering what options he had given my concerns about Paolo.

"I know, I know. Paolo's not a suspect," I said.

What about snooping into Paolo's past, unofficially? I wondered. The image of Carol, my talented and resourceful administrative assistant, popped into my head. She likes Gerard and would want to help if she thought he was in trouble.

Since the Marvelous Marley World cruise line had hired Paolo, it might not be as simple for her to access his records. Not as simple as it would have been if we had employed him in the Food and Beverage Division, but not impossible either. It was still early enough to contact her. I was pondering the issue when I realized Jack had started speaking again.

"You can't even hold those blond hairs against him any longer. It's not just that he's no peroxide blond like the owner of those stray hairs. Maggie called me to say the ones she found in Abby Kinkaid's locker are a match to those already in evidence. They're Abby's, not Paolo's."

"Is that what's going on? Are we headed to the infirmary to meet with Maggie about evidence she picked up at the spa?" I had a sinking feeling that I was asking a ridiculous question even as the words came out of my mouth.

"We're meeting Maggie—and Bill. Not in the infirmary, but in Abby Kinkaid's cabin on Deck 6. Once Maggie had that match, she called Bill. As soon as he could do it, he took a team to Abby's cabin hoping to speak to her."

That sinking feeling worsened as the door to an elevator taking us back to Deck 6, for the second time today, slid open. Right before we stepped into it, my phone beeped. Jack held the door open while I checked my phone.

It was a text message from Max. My skin crawled even more than it had done when Paolo kissed my hand.

ON A STOPOVER IN HONOLULU. EXPECT YOU TO UPDATE ME ON THE INVESTIGATION BEFORE WE TAKE OFF. I NEED ANSWERS! MAX

Jack took one look at my face. "Max?"

"Yep. There's something very wrong about dealing with your boss on your honeymoon," I groused as I tried to avoid looking at that grinning Olly-Olly Octopus hovering above us. "Max needs answers, Jack."

"Don't we all," Jack said, pulling me into his arms as that elevator door shut behind us. Jack's kiss was the answer to all my questions, including why not run for it while we still could?

Imagine fantasizing about an escape from a cruise to the South Sea Islands? I thought. I even chuckled when I shared that idea with Jack. As we stepped from that elevator, my laughter fled.

"Please tell me you're not taking your one-week-wife to another murder scene on her honeymoon," I pleaded as we strode down the corridor to Abby Kinkaid's cabin.

"I can't say that for sure," Jack said. "You can wait out here in the hall if you'd prefer.

"With a knife-wielding, killer who has struck more than once already? No way!" I said as Jack knocked and the cabin door swung open. I gasped.

11 CABIN FEVER

Abby Kinkaid's cabin was a disaster. Either a fight had broken out or someone had demolished it during a search, or both. Blood on the mattress, now lying on the floor, suggested Abby or someone else might be injured.

"It's a mess, but there's no body," Maggie said as we stepped into the small stateroom and shut the door behind us. Bill snapped photos of the wreckage in that room. Items were upended, drawers removed from the dressers. Someone had tossed mirrors and pictures on the floor. Some lay on top of the mattress shoved off the bed. Both the mattress and box springs had been sliced open.

Thank goodness we had taken a moment

to leave those beautiful take-out boxes Gerard had prepared for us with the concierge. The butler assigned to our suite would pick them up and stash them in our suite. They didn't belong anywhere near the noxious fever that had possessed whoever destroyed this cabin. Jack handed me his dinner jacket.

After that, Jack went into action, helping Maggie collect prints from surfaces in the room using a makeshift kit he had created. He and Maggie did their best to pick through items without moving them around much, at least until Bill snapped a photo. They searched as systematically as they could in the debris, for clues as to who might have been responsible for the carnage.

Maggie swabbed the blood on the wall behind the bed and collected a small swatch of cloth from the mattress where blood drops had fallen.

"Nothing like the amount of blood we found this morning. Maybe the person angry enough to do this got careless. See?" She asked. "There's blood on the glass from this broken lamp. Careless," Maggie muttered, repeating herself as she placed shards of blood-smeared glass into a baggie.

"Careless works for me," Jack said. "More of a chance that we'll nab whoever did this."

Maggie and Jack picked up a few hairs from bedclothes and pillows on the floor. More blond hairs, but several that were darker.

"Tina's?" I asked.

"The longer ones, maybe, but we have a couple short enough that they could belong to a man," Jack responded.

"If we're lucky, Abby yanked them out by the roots, and we'll get the follicles, too," Bill commented.

Ick, I thought. I got his point, but it was still gross. I felt almost claustrophobic as I tried to stay in a corner, out of the way. I did not want to get the powder they were using to dust for prints on my dress. Nor did I relish the idea of bumping into something that had blood on it, although the colorful floral print might provide camouflage if I did.

At least it was cool in this air-conditioned cabin. Unlike that murder scene out in the open air, this room could be left much as it was when we found it. There was less risk that the biological evidence would degrade fast, as it had done outside.

"Tropical heat, even in January, isn't helpful to crime scene preservation," Jack had said when we were back in our suite dressing for dinner.

The tent hadn't helped matters, either. While it kept passengers from stumbling across a vacation memory that would last a lifetime, it was getting hot in there by the time they finished evaluating that crime scene. Once they had documented the scene, preserved the evidence, and moved the body to the ship's morgue, they had cleaned up the area to avoid another problem—a biohazard on a ship crowded with adults and children.

"Didn't anyone report noise coming from in here? That blood could mean there was a fight, even if most of the carnage in this room is from a search," I asked.

"No. The blood is fresh, so this happened recently. Most of the passengers were likely up on Deck 2 eating dessert. The Captain says Chef Gerard has outdone himself and it's one of the biggest turnouts for an event on any cruise."

"They must have been searching for

valuables in Abby's possession. The safe in the back of her closet's open, but empty. Have you checked that area already?"

"Yes. It's one of the first things we did as soon as we made sure Abby wasn't in here— dead or alive," Bill said.

"No personal items or luggage around. Do you think Abby was all packed and ready to go when her visitor or visitors decided to ransack the room before dragging her out of here?" I asked.

"More likely, Abby did the same thing that Tina did. We can check but I bet Abby packed up, left, and had the steward assigned to her cabin clean it," Jack said.

"That must mean Tina and Abby decided to go undercover either before they set that plan into motion to have Perroquet run us down, or as soon as they found out how badly it went," I said.

"That makes sense in Tina's case because Justin could identify her. He'd gone to her cabin to find Martin Santo and again when he picked up that stupid parrot costume," Maggie said. "Why would Abby run? Justin never saw the two women together, did he?"

"It didn't take us that much effort to put the two women together. Even if we hadn't suspected there was a connection between Tina and Abby before we went to the spa, I'll bet Kayla or one of the other attendants would have made the connection for us. Ask about how to find Tina, and you get a lead to Abby," I replied.

"It could be," Jack muttered. "News sure gets around on this cruise—and fast. For Tina to steal that costume and recruit Justin, she must have picked us out as targets soon after we started asking questions."

"Well, someone had already warned Gerard. Maybe my visit to him triggered her interest in me, and she went into action. I must have been on my way to lunch with Gerard when Tina used that as an opportunity to set the scene for Justin. That's the only time Gerard and I were out on deck together."

"Yeah, well that's my point. You hadn't been with Gerard more than an hour or so before Tina stole that Perroquet costume and started working on Justin to get him to discourage you from any further snooping. Someone called Tina while Justin was in her cabin, setting his attack into motion. We were being watched by then for sure since Justin knew precisely where to find us." Before he could say more, Maggie interrupted and got us refocused on the present melee.

"So, let's say both women went into hiding, why come back here in the last hour or two?" Maggie asked.

"Abby had something Tina or that third man wanted back. Whatever double-dealing set all this in motion this morning hasn't been settled. If the blood is Abby's, either she wasn't cooperative, or they didn't find what they were looking for and took it out on her. The sooner we find them, the better chance Abby has of living through this. Any idea where else to search?" Jack asked. "What about the crew's quarters?"

"Well, they don't show up on video collected today at the main entry points to areas that are off limits to passengers. It's not like the cameras elsewhere on the ship that are fixed to capture a wide angle and leave gaps in coverage. At our core checkpoints, no one gets through without leaving a clear video record. At access points to the bridge, the engine room, crew quarters, and other sensitive restricted areas, we don't just record what goes on. We have eyes on them, too, using CCTV—closed circuit TV. We can reposition cameras or zoom in for a close-up. I had the video in those locations double-checked just in case someone missed something because this has been such a demanding day for security. Anyway, we can rule out those restricted areas as a place for Tina and Abby to hide out."

"Even if you're right about that, Bill, someone on the crew must be mixed up in this if it turns out Passenger X was a stowaway. If Georgie's right and Jake Nugent's killer used a fillet knife, it must have come from one of the kitchens, even though we haven't located it yet. The disarray Gerard found in the commissary kitchen means more than one crew member is involved if he's correct that a dispute between employees created that mess. Not to mention that the nasty message someone left for Gerard, using a dead duck to make the point, occurred in the crew quarters."

"I understand what you're saying, and I'm concerned about it too. Even with help from employees, if our passengers entered the restricted areas, we would have captured their images on video."

"Then where are Tina and Abby?" Jack

asked as he stood and removed the gloves that he had been wearing.

"Justin is young and not too bright, but there are a surprising number of men on cruises who can be taken in by a woman like Tina Marston. Abby, too, maybe. They could be in another passenger's stateroom. It's possible someone noticed a man with one of the women when they left their cabins rolling their luggage behind them. We're making the rounds asking about that now—among other things. Here on Deck 6 and above us on Deck 7 near the cabin assigned to Tina. We have a security team going cabin by cabin, with pictures of the two women, Jake Nugent, and Martin Santo."

"Martin Santo? Why?" I asked.

"I should have mentioned this when I called Jack a few minutes ago. When we had the sketch artist sit down with Justin and draw a picture of Martin Santo, it resembled the one we already had. We showed Justin the first drawing from Wendy Cutler and David Engels' descriptions of the third man they saw running away this morning. Justin got real excited. 'That's him! He must have ripped off other passengers, too, huh?'" Bill shook his head before going on. "Ya think? We had told him more than once that Martin Santo, if that's his real name, probably had a ring in his possession that wasn't his. Box of rocks."

"Stupid doesn't necessarily make him any less dangerous," Jack said.

"That is true. I'm glad Justin didn't hurt you and Georgie any worse than he did."

"Let's say Martin Santo is the third man in that fight this morning—a dark-haired, left-handed slasher who used what might have been a fillet knife to kill Jake Nugent. He's not on the passenger manifest. How can that be?" I asked.

"Who knows if that's even his real name? If he booked the cruise using another name, he could be sitting tight in his cabin right now. Tina and Abby could be with him," Bill replied.

"Not necessarily by choice, for Abby, given the disaster in this room," Maggie said as she pointed to a tiny object on the floor. "Can you get a photo of this before I bag it, please, Bill?" Bill did as she asked.

"What is that?" I asked Maggie.

"I'm not sure." Holding the item up for

closer inspection as she dropped it into a plastic baggie. "It's part of an earring or some other piece of jewelry. Not a real gem."

"There was a stone missing from that fake necklace Jake Nugent had on him, wasn't there?" I asked.

"More than one, as I recall," Jack replied.

"Yes," Maggie said. Maggie tagged the bag containing that fake gem. Then she got down on her knees and peered under the bed. "Maybe there are more like that under here."

"Bingo!" she cried a moment later. "I'm going to need a fresh glove and a bigger bag."

ANNA CELESTE BURKE

12 NO HONOR AMONG THIEVES?

"Abby may have had a male companion after all," Maggie said as she bagged and tagged what appeared to be a man's shoe.

"One who was at our murder scene," Jack added. "I hate to jump to conclusions, but the waffle-weave on the sole looks like a match to the print we found near Jake Nugent. It's distinctive."

"That's an overshoe—a shoe cover like you wear if you're working in slippery areas of a kitchen where there's water or grease. It's non-skid, easy to get on and off, and washable, too. You might not find much blood on it," I said.

"Easy off might explain why we didn't find more than one footprint. If Martin Santo

166

saw that print, he might have removed it before running away and leaving more tracks for us to follow." Jack leaned in to get a closer look at that shoe as he spoke.

"It's squishy," Maggie said, squeezing the plastic bag a little. "I guess that's how it got shoved up against the back wall under the bed."

I stood there, gazing at yet another link to the jewel thieves who seem to be behind all the horrible events of the day, including that murder. The silliest of concerns pounced upon my overtaxed brain as it ran a super-fast video replaying all that ugliness.

My feet hurt! I grumbled silently to myself. Everyone in this cabin had to be as exhausted and discouraged as me. How petty to worry about sore feet! Why had I worn heels?

Jack caught my eye and smiled, providing an immediate answer to that unspoken question. I'd worn the heels, the dress, and the lovely pendant I held between my fingers for Jack. Remembering, now, the way he had reacted when I stepped out of our bedroom, endorphins rushed through my body, soothing my aching feet.

"Georgie Shaw, you are a delight to

behold," he had exclaimed when he looked up from the laptop he held. His fingers had been moving rapidly over the keyboard, working on that report he was putting together compiling details about the investigation into the murder of Jake Nugent. Plus, notes about circumstances surrounding the man overboard, jewelry thefts, and our encounter with a giant parrot. Jack sat in a comfortable oversized chair with a Siamese cat perched on each arm of the chair, supervising his efforts.

"I'm glad you can say that after the day we've had," I had responded as I moved the laptop he was using to the coffee table in front of him. Their supervision no longer required, the cats took off. I slipped onto Jack's lap and wrapped my arms around him. "You work too hard, Detective. Some honeymoon, huh?"

"What are you saying? An adventure in the South Sea Islands is what I call a honeymoon to remember. None of this is your fault, but I had no doubt from the moment I saw you that life with you would be an adventure!"

"You're just saying that because I had a giant Persian cat in my clutches, at the base of Catmmando Mountain, on my way to a crime scene."

"Zing! Cupid's arrow struck on Valentine's Day in Arcadia Park earning the right to Max's claim that it's the most marvelous place on earth. You made my point exactly!"

"I doubt adventure would have come to mind if we'd met in my office with me sitting behind my desk reviewing budgets or writing mundane memos."

"I've been in your office when more than that was going on. An adventure there too."

"Hmm. That is true," I had said. "Maybe we should skip dinner and dessert and hang a do not disturb sign on the door. We've had plenty of adventure for one day, don't you agree?" My kiss had been convincing if I say so myself.

Jack's a man of duty, however. An alert on that laptop had stolen the moment, so to speak. I had opened an email from Bill containing a photo of Marsha Steven's necklace, and then leapt from Jack's lap. Not at the image of that necklace, but at the price tag on a claim form she filed with Captain Andrews along with the incident report. I moved out of the way so Jack could see the information on that laptop screen, too.

"Wow! My eye for pricey shiny things is even better than I realized. Why would anyone bring such an expensive piece of jewelry on a cruise? Although, I'm not sure where else you would wear it—a ball at Fort Knox or the crowning of a king. What could she be thinking?"

"I asked her that when I interviewed her."

"When did you do that?" I asked.

"While you were lounging in the tub. I told you I had a couple of loose end to tie up."

"Writing reports is what I heard." I shrugged. "So, what did she say?" I asked.

"This probably won't surprise you in the least. 'If you've got it, darling, flaunt it. Besides, it's insured.' It's not a museum piece, as she also pointed out when I pressed her on its value—which she hemmed and hawed about, I might add. Maybe, because I wasn't alone."

"Oh, so that 'darling' wasn't for you?" I had been teasing him a little when I used a vamp voice on that word darling, but I had also felt a bit relieved. "You're pretty smart, copper, not to venture into that moll's lair all alone."

"Adam took the original report from her, so it made sense to take him with me."

My Jack is a man of logic. The relief I had felt earlier washed over me again as I stood there waiting for this latest episode in our adventure to be over. I'm not sure why it had bothered me that he might have met with Marsha Stevens alone. I had known before I married him that my one-week-husband was a savvy, seasoned detective, not easy prey for vamps or villains.

What is my problem? I wondered as I stood idly by watching the other three people in the room work. Have I suddenly become a jealous woman? I've never thought of myself in that way before. Maybe not all the changes that go with love and marriage are good ones. Jack is a man of integrity. Then again, I hope I'm as trustworthy as he is, and yet Paolo's flirtation had bothered him. Jealousy goes with the territory in matters of the heart—even at our age.

Under the right—or wrong—circumstances, jealousy can be lethal. Maybe that story of infidelity Tina made up casting me in the role of Jezebel hadn't been a complete fabrication. Had Martin Santo betrayed Tina with Abby?

"Can you imagine being a member of this team of thieving rogues? How would you ever be able to trust each other? Two very attractive women and the men who love to steal stuff with them. Only barely believable as the plot for a movie. Real life is stranger than fiction, though, isn't it?" I asked, still wondering if the betrayal among these thieves was about more than business. Maggie's thoughts must have been moving along the same track.

"Yeah, but you forgot to add a line about 'Until something goes terribly wrong and their love turns to hatred.' Even harder to believe, I know, but something has set this pack of wild dogs loose on each other," Maggie commented. "I hope we can find them before they kill again—even if it's one of the wild dogs in the pack who's at risk."

"There's no honor among this bunch of thieves," I added. "Why not add two-timing to double-dealing as a motive for murder and mayhem? Maybe Tina tore this room apart looking for proof that Martin Santo had been in here. What if she found the mate to that shoe and took it with her? It's not in here, Jack."

"Whether this is about greed or love turned to hatred, Maggie's right that we need to catch up with them. So far, they've managed to keep a step ahead of us. How hard can it be to figure out where they're hiding on a ship at sea?"

"Before you ask, Jack. Yes, we reviewed footage from the video camera in the corridor near Tina's room. She left this morning, at the crack of dawn, wearing workout gear, and so did Abby. If the report you got from the spa is correct, they never made it there."

"Yes, that's true, but Justin says Tina was back in her cabin a couple of hours later with that parrot costume. From what Kayla told us at the spa, Tina was capable of lugging that thing to her cabin from wherever she stole it. A woman carrying around a huge parrot costume is going to stand out. Surely that got picked up on a camera somewhere."

"You must have some idea, Jack, of how much footage that is. We can't possibly go through all of it in a short time, so we pick and choose what to review based on location and timing. What we found is a snippet of film showing a man wheeling away two large, bulky sacks near an exit from that theater. We assume the costume was in them. They could have passed for garbage bags if anyone had even noticed. It could be Martin Santo, but the man is wearing sunglasses and a hoodie, keeps his head down, and then steps out of range of that camera as soon as he can. Whoever it is seems way too careful to be box-of-rocks-Justin."

"Sounds like someone who's familiar enough with the surveillance system to play games with you, Bill."

"It gets worse, Jack, when it comes to playing games. We don't have any more video of Tina Marston later in the day because someone covered the lens on the camera in the corridor near her cabin."

"Don't you get an alert when a camera goes offline?" Jack asked.

"Technically, it wasn't offline. It was still recording, but blocked because someone put peanut butter on it."

"Peanut butter?" Jack and I asked almost at the same time. Bill nodded.

"I thought I caught a whiff of peanut

butter in the corridor on our way here. Does that mean we have no video of what went on here, either?" Jack asked.

"Yes, I'm afraid so. The ship's relatively new, and it's the first time we've had to put the video equipment to the test. There was a housekeeping cart in the hall on Deck 7 not long before someone monkeyed with the lens. We spoke to the steward on duty then who says she cleaned Tina's cabin, but never saw Tina or Justin or anyone else hauling a big, bulky sack down the hall."

"Nothing on any of the images from cameras in the elevators or aimed at public spaces nearby on Decks 6 and 7?" Jack asked.

"No," Bill replied. "Lots of passengers and crew come and go, but none of our culprits and no one hauling garbage bags on or off an elevator.

"How is that possible?" Jack asked. He was clearly frustrated at the thieves' ability to elude detection. There was more than a little irritation in his tone.

"If I knew, I'd tell you," Bill replied, in an equally irritated manner.

Silence fell over us again. I didn't want

to add to the uncomfortable feeling that had settled in amidst that silence, but another unresolved issue bubbled up in my mind.

"Just so I'm clear about this. If Martin Santo is the third man Wendy Cutler and David Engels spotted this morning, he's our killer and not Passenger X. So, in addition to Martin Santo who's a passenger on board using a name that's not on the manifest, there's still the matter of an unidentified man overboard. That means there are two passengers unaccounted for on that manifest. Any progress figuring that one out?" I tried not to hyperventilate as I imagined Max asking that question. *Maybe the cabin fever that struck in here is contagious*, I thought as I tried to calm myself down.

After more than twenty-five years of Max's tantrums, I was more afraid for him than I was of him. I'd play the retirement card the moment he got out of line with me. Jack didn't work for him so good luck pulling that Ari'i nui routine with Detective Wheeler.

No, what I dreaded was the melodramatic scene he would make. I did not relish the prospect of watching Mad Max's face turn ashen with excessive grief, smacking his head in disbelief at his team's failure.

"Why, why, why me?" he had lamented on more than one occasion. As he paced in circles, I had braced myself for that moment when he would rend his garments in anger and despair. It hadn't happened yet, but two unidentified passengers—one overboard and the other a slasher roaming loose on his newest, top of the line cruise ship—just might do it. Oh yeah, there was also the matter of stolen jewelry and two women who were on the passenger manifest but have since vanished.

Worse even than Max's woe-is-me victim act was this awful shade of purple he turned when he got in touch with his inner Rumpelstiltskin. His eyes wild and bulging, his fists balled up, writhing, and jumping up and down, he bore an even greater resemblance to Olly-Olly. Not a healthy thing for a man in his seventies, who worked eighty hours a week and consumed way too much junk food.

"Max wants answers, guys. What am I going to tell him?" My question hung like an ax waiting to fall in the silence that filled the cabin. "Would it be wrong just to ignore the message and pretend I didn't get it until morning?" I wondered aloud. A resounding round of "nos" broke the silence.

I wanted to believe them. The theme from Jaws pounded in my head, though, as I imagined Max closing in on our ship like a Great White or a giant squid. By morning, he'd be in Tahiti—way too close for comfort. Why put off my encounter with the Big Chief? I began to compose a message to Max as I waited for Jack and the others to finish their work. I reminded Max about how good Jack is at his job, but he had to give him and the others involved in the investigation more time. Max had been so grateful that we'd solved the mystery surrounding the disappearance of his leading lady in the remake of The Lonely Swan Prince. The actress portraying Princess Christiana seemed to have vanished into thin air from her dressing room at Max Marley Studios. When I had put that into a message, I hit send.

IT'S ALL-HANDS-ON-DECK HERE. INVESTIGATION STILL ONGOING. YOU KNOW HOW WELL JACK HANDLED CHRISTIANA'S DISAPPEARANCE. GIVE THE DETECTIVE TIME TO WORK HIS MAGIC. BESIDES, HE HAS ME AT HIS SIDE. WHAT MORE COULD YOU WANT? SEE YOU IN TAHITI.

I sighed when I heard that whoosh

sound. Suddenly, an image of a coffee cart in the hallway near the vanishing actress's dressing room resonated with what Bill had said about a laundry cart in the corridor near Tina's cabin.

"Bill, could the costume have fit into that laundry cart left outside Tina's stateroom?"

"Probably, but there's still no sign of Tina or that hoodie-wearing man we picked up on video earlier near the theater exit. We looked for him. Lots of people are coming and going, but none of the ones we're looking for."

"Where does that cart go when they've finished cleaning the cabins?" I asked."

"The Stateroom Stewards use dedicated elevators that take them down to the laundry where they can dump the soiled linens and towels or drop off personal items guests leave in the small laundry bags found in each stateroom."

"Are those elevators under surveillance, too?"

"Yes. Not on CCTV like the access points to more sensitive restricted areas. We've reviewed the recorded footage from those cameras. There's no sign of passengers forcing their way onto the crew elevators or stewards allowing members of this pack of wild dogs onto them."

I relented. Still, I couldn't let go of the idea that the wild dogs appeared to have the run of the ship. The thieves knew their way around the kitchen, the theater, and were familiar with the location of surveillance cameras. It takes moxie to tamper with those cameras and craftiness to get away with it unless they had help from the crew.

Max is going to have to wait until tomorrow to hear this from me, I thought. I was glad I had already sent him a message before I hit bottom as Jack and Bill had done when they got caught up in that stressful interaction. Who could blame them?

13 PEARLS IN A BOTTLE

Jack and I escorted Maggie back to the infirmary with the evidence collected from the devastation in that cabin. Maggie checked the blond hairs and concluded they were a good match for those obtained from Abby's locker. Little else seemed to be of immediate value, other than that overshoe and the gem Maggie had found.

Photos on Maggie's computer of the fake necklace confirmed that the gem was one of those missing from the bad copy of Marsha Steven's expensive piece of jewelry. Another photo revealed the sole of the shoe was a perfect match to the markings in that print found near Jake Nugent. Maybe the fingerprints they had also collected would turn out to be of value. Who knew?

Dog-tired, we headed back up to Deck 2 toward the adult end of the ship where The Captain's Table was located. Nearby, was the Pearls in a Bottle Lounge—the bar where Justin claimed to have met Martin Santo for the first time.

"We still have a few minutes before dinner. Feel like having a toast to surviving day 8 of our honeymoon, Jack?"

"Why not? That is something to celebrate, isn't it?"

Hawaiian music was playing softly in the background as the hostess led us to a secluded booth toward the back of the beautifully appointed bar and lounge. The room glowed with backlit glass tiles in various shades of aqua lining the walls in wavy strips. Above them, milky white tiles mimicked the frothy waves that rolled onto the nearby beaches. The wall behind the bar was lit too, with tiny bubbles floating upward, accenting bottles on glass shelves.

The bubbles appeared to be moving through real water, unlike a similar display on the walls in our suite. Ella had been happily chasing bubbles rather than fish when we returned to our suite yesterday. Our ingenious cats had not only figured out how to activate the images on that wall but had changed them.

The butler who had introduced us to the "Marveling Wall" when he demonstrated the technological wonders of our suite, assured us that he had not changed the video display. I hid the remote but left the motion-activated sensors on. Ella enjoyed it so much. Miles got a break, too, if Ella ran herself ragged chasing things that moved on the wall rather than him.

Maybe Ella knew what she was doing. Those bubbles were mesmerizing. It could have been that my brain was turning to mush after the day we'd had. Or maybe I was just grateful that the décor in here was so pleasant and relaxing and devoid of Marvelous Marley World characters.

"Here's to no sign of Penelope, Perroquet, or Olly-Olly anywhere," I said. Not waiting for our champagne to arrive, I used the water our hostess had poured after seating us to make that toast.

"No tiki-tiki song playing in the background, either. Cheers, one-week-wife!"

"What a day, one-week-husband. Any idea what is going on?"

"I'm working on it. No sign of the murder weapon, although there could be a fillet knife missing from the kitchen. As you suggested, Adam and I checked."

"Don't tell me. While I was in the tub, right?" I asked.

"Yep," Jack replied.

"And you called me unstoppable," I said. "_Could_ be a knife missing—what does that mean?"

"I don't need to tell you what goes on in a busy kitchen. Gerard and Paolo's personal knives are easy to track down, and we've accounted for them. The poissonnier—fish chef—was insulted that we even thought his knife could be missing. It didn't help that I'd never heard of a fish chef before. When he cooled down, he admitted that he wasn't sure how many fillet knives were in his area of the commissary kitchen. Most kitchen staff don't use them elsewhere, but with so many kitchens on this ship, who knows? Sometimes less well-trained kitchen staff grab the wrong knife and take off with it."

"Does Gerard back him up on that?"

"Yes. Gerard said he couldn't be sure where the knife had come from that had been used to stab that raw duck left outside his door. Most likely, a knife from the commissary since it was a boning knife, but he agreed that knives 'migrate' from one place to another on board."

"Well, that's a lot of potential suspects if not only commissary kitchen staff but crew members in the galley kitchens were able to get their hands on the knife used to kill Jake Nugent."

"Not just kitchen staff, Georgie, but anyone who passed through those areas, like waiters, expediters, stewards picking up room service items," Jack shook his head. "It's discouraging to get information that widens our search rather than narrowing it.

"I'm sorry, Jack. I get your point. It's like the proverbial needle in a haystack to pick out the thieves' accomplices from among the crew when there are hundreds to choose from."

"Too many cooks and crooks in the mix for the time being. All our primary suspects like to shop, too. That plastic we found could have come from several shops on board. So far, purchases from Tina, Abby, Jake, and Justin have all turned up at stores that use bags made from that plastic. The only oddity that stands out is that Jake Nugent's purchases included a few items more likely to be found on a woman's shopping list than that of a single man on a cruise alone. Maybe he had something going on with one of his thieving partners as you suggested when we were in Abby's trashed stateroom."

"What sort of items?"

"Nail polish, nail polish remover, and a nail-mending kit. Cotton swabs and baby powder—stuff like that."

"Was it clear nail polish?" I asked.

"Yes. Why?"

"Clear nail polish can be used for all sorts of things. In high school, we used it to stop a run in our stockings from getting worse. I've used it to prevent an eyeglass screw from falling out of my sunglasses. I don't know if Jake could have used it to keep those loose gems in place on that necklace, or maybe there's an adhesive in that mending kit that could have done that. My mom used to put clear nail polish on her costume jewelry to keep it from tarnishing, I don't know if it could have secured loose gems."

"That's helpful to know, Georgie."

"Just don't ask me what a big Texas jewelry salesman would be doing with baby powder, so maybe you're right that there's a woman involved."

"We did find that loose gem in Abby's cabin, so maybe Jake Nugent had been there. If Martin Santo wasn't the only man in her life on board this cruise that could have made things even more complicated," Jack offered.

"If she was involved with both Jake Nugent and Martin Santo that could explain why Martin Santo slit Jake Nugent's throat this morning."

"Could be. The guy they tossed overboard before they turned on each other could have been another of Abby's suitors if she was working all the men in the theft ring. We still don't know what Jake was doing with that fake necklace. Maybe he and Abby were planning to replace the stolen necklace with the phony one and keep the original—or already had the original, and that's what that search was about."

"Well on a ship with a man overboard and no missing passenger—why not a stolen necklace that gets stolen a second time? It fits with the notion that the murder and mayhem is about double-dealing. Tina must have found it, since we didn't when we went through Abby's cabin. Or it was never in there in the first place. How did Tina miss that gem and that shoe?"

"That seems odd to me. The gem is tiny, so I could see her missing that or leaving it behind. That shoe's another matter. Maybe you had it right when you said this is about two-timing as well as double-dealing. Maybe she found the mate and left the other one behind. If all she was out to do was prove that Martin Santo had been unfaithful, finding one of his shoes in that cabin would have done the job. She had to be in a bigger hurry than we were and, if that cabin is any indication of Tina's state of mind, she could not have been thinking clearly."

"Or, maybe she found the necklace before she got around to checking for anything under the bed. At least you all got to Jake Nugent's cabin before anyone else did. You searched it, didn't you?"

"Yes—not the way Tina, or someone else,

searched Abby's cabin. Bill secured Jake Nugent's cabin immediately this morning. His luggage was still there, and we went through that thoroughly. No real necklace or fake gems. No nail polish or baby powder or any of that stuff, either, even though we didn't know we were looking for those items, then. I'm confident we would have noticed anything that suggested a woman had been in that cabin. The only person caught on film going in or out of that room in addition to Jake Nugent, was room service and the ship's steward bringing fresh towels and cleaning up."

"Without the dead bodies, this would almost be comical. Not very stealthy to create as much commotion as they have on this ship and yet they remain hidden. They're everywhere and nowhere all at once."

"I agree. Not the most professional gang of thieves. Yet, getting their hands on Marsha Stevens' necklace without her noticing it was being taken was a slick move."

"A big score for amateurs, too, if that's what they are. I still don't get why Marsha Stevens would risk wearing a quarter-million-dollars' worth of jewelry on a cruise. Even though she still has the earrings, that necklace was a big loss. I haven't seen the list Bill gave you of all the missing and stolen jewelry items. If the tennis bracelet and engagement ring are indications of what they steal, that necklace has to be worth more than the rest combined even including the expensive watches lifted from men at the spa."

"I have seen the list, and you are correct." Jack had more to say, but our hostess returned with two glasses of champagne and a couple of oysters. Those oysters weren't meant to be eaten. Apart from the excellent wine list with several fine wines in a category they called "Bottled Pearls," the establishment's claim to fame was oysters guaranteed to contain a pearl. Cultured pearls, to be sure, but still a charming souvenir of a cruise to the South Seas.

"On the house," she said as she set those oysters down with our drinks. "Happy honeymoon!" Then she went to work, opening those oysters in front of us.

"What a pleasant surprise," I said.

"Wow, these are beauties!" she exclaimed a couple of minutes later. She held each one up, then rinsed, and dried them before slipping them into a tiny velvet bag. "Can I bring you anything else?"

"Champagne and pearls are perfect," I replied. "Thank you so much."

"Thank you," Jack added. "We'll have to take off for dinner in a few minutes. Will you need anything else from us?"

"No, we swiped your card when you came in, so you're all set."

"I have a quick question. What do you do if you seat a guest who doesn't have a card with them?"

"I'd apologize, but I wouldn't seat them until they went and got it," she replied. "Those cards make sure no one can charge to the wrong cabin—accidently or on purpose. Part of the fantasy on MMW's Fantasy of the Sea is the cashless world. Hopefully, that means less worry about money during the trip. All-inclusive means just that—if you opt for that package. Convenient, huh?" our waitress asked.

"Marvelous," I said. "What else would you expect from MMW Fantasy of the Sea?"

"Just keep that card handy, and all your dreams can come true," she said picking up the items she'd used to serve us.

Jack wasn't ready to let her go quite yet.

"Is there any way someone could be seated here, or at the bar, and drinking without a card with them?"

Our hostess thought about that for a moment. "Well, if they came in with someone else—like the two of you—only one member of the party has to have a card with them. Is that what you're asking?"

"Yes," Jack nodded, and then muttered, "I think so." In a louder voice, he thanked our hostess, and she slipped away.

"You're thinking about Justin's encounter with Martin Santo, aren't you?"

"Yes. It's possible that Justin was telling us the truth. Since Martin Santo doesn't show up on the passenger manifest, he couldn't have had a key card. If he had already started drinking before Justin sat down, he must have had another companion picking up the tab before he bummed drinks from Justin."

"All the transactions in here are time-stamped, I'm sure. You might be able to identify his earlier drinking companion."

"You're right. I'll ask Bill for the names of other passengers who bought drinks an hour or so before Justin made his first purchase.

Maybe we'll find a name we recognize."

"Or a new one that matters, Jack."

"That's possible, too, although we need more suspects like we need a hole in the head," Jack said.

"I was wondering about that. This series of escapades is like a less well-organized version of the operation in that Ocean's Eleven movie where they robbed the casino. Three men in the fight this morning, two women passengers helping lift jewelry, plus at least two crew members if Gerard's right that more than one person was involved in disputes in the commissary. That's seven people already, and Justin makes eight."

"Yeah, not all that surprising that they've started killing each other if you look at it that way, is it?" Jack asked. "Too many mouths to feed, even with that bonanza they scored stealing that necklace."

"Or maybe because of that windfall. To some people that necklace may look like a ticket out of thievery. This could have become a game of winner-takes-all."

"Which may also mean more bodies yet to come, Georgie. Whoever helped shove that man overboard and then killed Jake Nugent reduced the number of contenders for a share early this morning. Eight has gone down to six just like that!" Jack snapped his fingers for emphasis.

"It's an even bigger chunk for each of the remaining members of the ring if they're using hired hands, like Justin, and not everyone expects a cut. Their paid help may not even understand what they're mixed up in if they're no brighter than their patsy sitting in the brig."

"Bill seems to think unwitting passengers like Justin are easy to find on a cruise like this one. It had to be a crew member who gave them information about the surveillance system on board. Grabbing that Perroquet costume required familiarity with what goes on in that theater. Getting away with covering those camera lenses was tricky too. Slipping a few bucks to hired hands may reduce the number of people expecting a cut of the loot, but it increases the number of people who can get in the way or give them away, like Justin. I'm convinced there's a crew member doing double-duty as part of this theft ring."

"I hear you, Jack."

"Crew members aren't allowed to drink

with the passengers, from what I understand. Reviewing the transactions at the bar won't help if that's the case."

"Some staff members can fraternize, I believe. Ask Bill when you call him about getting that list of sales transactions from the bar. They must flag charges to staff accounts. It ought to at least be easy to figure out if anyone from the ship's crew was in here while Martin Santo was drinking his sorrows away at the bar."

"If that's what he was doing. Who knows why he was flashing that stolen engagement ring around." Jack shook his head as he sipped champagne. "Drunks are as bad as amateurs."

"Drowning his sorrows might be what he was doing if he was the two-timer involved in a romantic triangle with Tina and Abby, and got caught. That would make more sense, though, if he'd been the one who ended up overboard or dead on Deck 6."

"Not necessarily if Abby was doing to him what he was doing to Tina Marston. Martin Santo could have been angry enough to take out the other two men with him this morning if this is about jealousy. That fake necklace in Jake Nugent's possession must mean there's more than one kind of hanky-panky going on. Martin Santo had to be out of the loop or he would never have left it behind. That tied the murder and the thefts together from the very beginning."

"Marsha Stevens can't help you make any connection between her and Jake Nugent? There must be one for him to have brought that fake necklace with him on this cruise," I argued, as my suspicions shifted back to her.

"Marsha Stevens says no. She claims she never met the man—not even on this cruise. If he was among the men in that crowd you saw around her at the bar, he didn't make a lasting impression because she doesn't remember bumping into him there. I believe her. You had your eye on her and that necklace, I'm sure you would have noticed if the dead guy on Deck 6 was one of her suitors that night."

"Jake Nugent was a big man—I could tell that even when he was sprawled on the ground. None of the guys at the bar with Marsha Stevens stood out in the height department. Still, Jake was well-connected to the jewelry business. He certainly would have known someone capable of making a knockoff. Could he have had a copy made and shipped to him to pick up at one of our stops along the way?"

"You spotted it as a fake right away, so it wasn't the highest quality copy. Maybe that's because it was a rush job. I can't conceive of any way they could have gotten a copy made and on board this ship in less than a week, though. If we were back in the OC, I'd have a bunch of colleagues to consult. With a few more days, I'd have time to find out things like how fast a copy of a piece of jewelry can be made. We'd be able to run more thorough background checks on these hooligans to see if the ones we can identify have crossed paths before—including the owner of that necklace who's still a person of interest. It's even more unfortunate that our list of suspects is still incomplete if it's also true that we're looking for an unknown number of crew members. What's more frustrating is that we can't locate any of the known suspects within the confined space of this ship. Heck, we don't even know the identity of our second victim. We're running out of time, and the only good news about that is that the thieves only have a little more time to kill each other before this ship docks in Tahiti."

"I understand, Jack. I'm feeling the

pressure from Max and the FBI breathing down our necks, so it's got to be worse for you. Time running out isn't all bad. In another day or two at the most, we'll just be a newly married couple on the next leg of our honeymoon. Good riddance, I say, whether this has all been figured out or not."

"I'll drink to that, Georgie, my love," Jack added, giving my glass a little clink. "Let me call Bill and then let's go have dinner and then we'll call it a day, okay?"

In my mind, I imagined an enormous clock. Instead of wishing that it would slow down, I willed it to speed up! Tomorrow, when we arrived at Bora Bora we'd turn this whole nightmare over to the FBI. Let Max tell them he needs answers when he struts on deck in Tahiti. By then, we'll have shared all we know with the investigative team taking over the case. With our job done, we can wave as we run for it—off this ship just as Max is coming aboard.

"Aah!" I said feeling like I could breathe again for the first time since that text message from Max.

14 NOT A BORA BORA

It was eight o'clock on the dot when we finally arrived at The Captain's Table. The small, exquisite dining spot only seated guests twice each night—6:00 and 8:00. We had expected to be late to our dinner at six because of that dessert-fest, but even being fashionably late became an impossibility once we caught up with Bill and Maggie at Abby Kinkaid's cabin. At 6:30, I had given up and called to cancel our reservation. The maître d' offered us a place at the later seating, and I took it, hoping to salvage some shred of day 8 of our honeymoon cruise, just for Jack and me.

A few minutes after our arrival, we sat at one of two elegantly appointed tables as a dozen guests settled in around us. No captain or captain's mate headed either table tonight. One sign that a search was still underway for a missing passenger. Usually, Gerard or another high-ranking chef, like Paolo, sat at the head of the second table. They were absent tonight, too, dealing with the upheaval from a change in the ship's routine.

Except for the wall of windows open to a view of the sea and the night sky, the dining room was paneled in polished exotic woods. It felt intimate. More like a library or a private dining room than a restaurant. Gleaming brass embellishments conveyed a nautical theme in a subtle way. On one wall, an ornate wood and glass cabinet housed the fine wines served with our dinner.

A flash of light caught my eye as a beam swept back and forth on the surface of the water. A second sign that this was no ordinary evening in a lavish dining room on a luxury cruise.

Subdued conversation ensued as the staff moved around us, pouring water and handing us menus with the limited options available featuring Chef Gerard's choices for the evening. That included recommendations for wine to accompany each course.

The French in French Polynesia was emphasized on the menu tonight. I wondered how much Gerard had counted on being able to put into port today to pick up supplies for this dinner. Could he possibly have all the fresh ingredients for a red and yellow beet carpaccio with walnuts, goat cheese, mesclun greens, in a balsamic vinaigrette? It made me tired just thinking about how much Gerard must have had to scramble to alter menu options given the sudden detour our cruise had taken. No wonder he wasn't around.

I ordered duck magret with fig and port sauce as my main dish—even though I had no doubt that Gerard's seafood feuillette had to be delicious. The lure of the puff pastry in that dish must have overcome my husband's usual preference for a well-prepared filet mignon. He had forgone the steak au poivre for the savory blend of fresh shrimp, scallops, and lobster served in a flaky pastry case. We both declined to order dessert given the binge we'd had earlier this evening. Plus, there were more goodies in those take-out boxes stowed away in our cabin.

I reached under the table and gave Jack's hand a squeeze. I hoped that would help put the more disagreeable sights of the day out of my mind. It worked.

"Newlyweds, aren't you?" The passenger seated on my right asked.

"Yes. How did you know?" She waited a moment to respond to my question. Our servers were back pouring the wine paired with our choice of appetizers. Once they had moved on to other guests at our table, she spoke up again.

"No big secret or anything. I'm Hetty Green," she said offering her hand for me to shake. "I overheard you talking to Chef Gerard when you were in here earlier this week." She leaned closer and in a quieter voice said, "I eat here every night. My husband, God rest his soul, was a ship's captain and I pull strings to make sure I'm a regular."

"How wonderful for you, Hetty. I'm Georgie Shaw, and this is my husband, Jack Wheeler."

"You're that detective, aren't you?" she asked without skipping a beat. I nearly fell off my chair. Jack appeared to be more composed as he shook the hand she had shoved under my nose.

"I am a detective, true. I'm not sure if

MURDER AT SEA OF PASSENGER X

I'm _'that'_ detective."

"Oh sure, sure, I know." She lowered her voice again, twisting in her seat to get closer before speaking, "I was told your investigation is hush-hush."

"Told, by whom?" I asked.

"I can't disclose my sources, now can I? I'm no stranger to the bridge or the crew there. My Harry and I were always welcome no matter what was going on. I'm still granted special privileges except when there's trouble like today. That doesn't mean they can send me packing without answering a question or two." Hetty paused to take a sip of the wine poured for her.

"Besides, I'm no fool when it comes to shipboard trouble. Oscar wasn't the only code word that went out over the speakers today. Here's a tip. If you see me scooting toward a lifeboat, follow me!"

"Will do! Let's hope it doesn't come to that," I said. Despite my shock at how much she knew about Jack and me, I liked Hetty Green immediately. The large, sturdy-looking senior citizen wore a bright Polynesian floral print, floor-length dress. More fitted than a muumuu or a caftan, it still seemed to flow about her as she sat down. That added to the breezy free-spirited vibe she exuded as she spoke.

"If you haven't taken a tour of the bridge you should. There's no place like it. Even better than a visit to the commissary."

My mouth opened. "You know about that too? How?"

"I take this cruise several times a year, so I have lots of friends on this ship. That includes the handsome and talented Chef Gerard. He thinks highly of you and your new husband. I would say he has excellent judgment, except that he can't seem to see through that phony Sous Chef who follows him around like a hound."

"You're not dazzled by all that old school continental charm?" Jack asked. I was a little surprised he had heard Hetty, given that the background buzz had increased in volume.

"Not for a minute. Paolo's got talent, don't get me wrong, but he's looking to move up in the world. If he can find a woman who's loaded like my friend, Marsha Stevens, he's out of here. Gerard will be left high and dry."

"Do you think it's the woman he's after or her wares?" Jack asked.

"Why not go for the goose rather than the golden egg?" she responded. "If what you're asking me is if I believe he's the one with the light touch who stole Marsha's pricey necklace, I don't think so. Shortsighted, too, if his aspirations are to live happily ever after with the woman of his dreams who also happens to have a bottomless purse."

Clearly, Jack had ventured beyond astonishment at Hetty's grasp of the intrigue afoot on this cruise. An apparently willing informant, she seemed eager to share what she knew. Jack was hooked on every word.

"Marsha's a repetitive cruiser, like me. She hasn't been around as long as I have, but she's wise beyond her years. That hound's barking up the wrong tree," Hetty laughed. Her laughter was infectious. I felt more lighthearted than I had all day.

"Too bad she lost that gorgeous piece of jewelry. I hope it doesn't change her mind about taking this cruise again in the spring. I enjoy her company when she's not hot on the trail of a man on board. Marsha's not out to marry for money like Paolo. Still, she's not shy about the fact that she enjoys the finer things in life, like the jewelry her ex-husband gave her. She says 'easy come, easy go,' but her story about what she went through before her divorce doesn't sound easy to me."

"I don't want to be nosy, Hetty, but has Marsha worn that necklace on cruises before?"

"Of course, she has! That necklace is a man magnet as if she needs it!" Hetty replied. "Please, be as nosy as you want. I hope you catch the perp—that's what you call them, right, Detective?"

"Yes, Hetty, on occasion we do call them that although we have a few other choice names for them too." Hetty laughed heartily at that. "Who do you think stole that necklace?" Jack asked.

"That drunk who bumped into her as she was leaving Neptune's Garden. Classic pickpocket routine—create a distraction, then a little misdirection, and presto it's gone!" Hetty rippled her fingers through the air. "Marsha doesn't believe me. The guy was three sheets to the wind and acted like he was going to fall after slamming into her. I'm sure while she steadied him, he clipped the chain or opened the clasp and slipped it off. She was so intent on getting the foul beast away from her, I doubt she would have noticed if he'd taken her earrings too."

"Did she get a good look at the man?" Jack asked.

"I'm not sure. Paolo turned up right about then. When he started making a fuss, asking if she was okay, the drunk took off—not running, but at a good clip for someone that drunk."

I glanced at Jack. The wheels were turning. Recounting every word of his conversation with Marsha Stevens, if I had to guess. Had she mentioned that encounter with a drunk? She claimed never to have seen Jake Nugent. What about Martin Santo or Justin Michelson? Both men had convinced that ship's steward they were drunk when they got caught in a scuffle on Deck 6. Had Martin Santo bumped into her and stolen her necklace? A question from a guest seated across from me intruded into my ruminations about Hetty's revelation.

"It's a shame Captain Andrews can't be with us tonight. He is such an interesting man, isn't he?" It wasn't evident to whom the gray-haired, bespectacled woman was speaking, but

Hetty responded.

"He's got his hands full searching for that missing passenger. No way can he leave the bridge under the circumstances."

"I still say it's a shame. Our one chance to eat at The Captain's Table and the Captain's not even here," said the elderly man sitting beside the woman who had asked that question about Captain Andrews.

"This whole trip has gotten so messed up. It's been one thing after another. I promised to bring something for my kids from every island on our itinerary. Now, what am I going to do?" asked a woman sitting at the opposite end of the table.

"Tell them something fishy happened on board," her companion snorted. "I for one don't mind all the changes. That free Olly-Olly dessert buffet was an 'unshellfish' act," the man added, emphasizing what he apparently regarded as another clever play on words.

"Uh-oh, a punster," I said under my breath.

"A bad one," Hetty added in a whisper.

The gentleman had more to say. "A

gesture of unfathomable depth, I was nearly swept overboard myself by the splashy Olly-Olly display. Kudos to Paolo, I must say," the fellow brayed.

A waiter across from me rolled his eyes ever so slightly as disgruntled guests moaned. He caught me looking at him and broadened the phony smile plastered on his face. I smiled in return even though I was aghast at the insensitivity in that passenger's last set of remarks.

"Tasteless, too," I told Hetty, quietly, "with a fellow passenger still lost at sea." Hetty nodded, but not everyone at the table must have shared my concern. The woman who had complained about Captain Andrews' absence spoke up.

"Extra desserts hardly make up for skipping an onshore excursion to a key destination on our itinerary," she sniffed indignantly.

"Or for the distressing day we've had, worrying about what was going to happen next," another passenger added.

"At least you can't say it's a Bora Bora," the "punster" quipped, then guffawed at his joke. Another round of groans came from passengers seated at our table.

"How much you want to bet he's the next guy shoved overboard?" Jack whispered. Hetty heard him and chuckled. "If you two delightful women will forgive me, I need to step out for a moment."

"Do you promise to hurry back?" I asked. Then, I leaned in and whispered in his ear. "You want Adam or Bill to show that picture of Martin Santo to Marsha Stevens, don't you?"

"Absolutely," he whispered. Then speaking loud enough for Hetty to hear, too, he said, "It pains me to leave you two alone for long."

"Not to mention that you don't want to insult Chef Gerard by letting his food get cold," Hetty chided. Jack nodded and took off, his phone already in his hand.

"More wine, Ma'am?" That waiter from the other side of our table asked.

"Yes, please," I replied as I watched Jack. He turned to look at me as he made that call. Bill Tate must have answered because Jack began speaking to someone.

I hoped Martin Santo was, indeed, the drunk who had bumped into Marsha Stevens. The possibility that some other drunk with expert pickpocket skills was roaming the ship was more than I could bear to consider. Still, what difference would it make if it had been Martin Santo unless we could find him?

15 MORNING CONSTITUTIONAL

I felt as though I had a hangover when I woke up on Day 9 of our ten-day voyage. Not from drinking, but from too many sweets. My chocoholism had done its worst. I had not been able to resist a peek at the treats in those take-out boxes when we finally returned to our cabin. A huge mistake. Even Jack had been unable to resist the urge to "eat dessert twice."

"Lucy and Ethel must have felt like this after they got fired from that job at the candy factory," I murmured. That Rumi quote about the sea breeze carrying secrets didn't help me get out of bed this morning. In fact, all the ugly secrets that we had uncovered yesterday made me want to pull the silky covers up over my head.

In addition to suffering the consequences of my overindulgence, I was feeling the aftermath of my wrestling match with that fool Justin. Why not stay here? I'd be comfy and safe from missing passengers which no one seemed to miss, murderous thieves, and a misguided youth all too willing to play the patsy.

When I became fully conscious, I suddenly remembered that my gorgeous little bauble had disappeared last night. Where? Jack and I couldn't be sure. Its disappearance was eerily like Marsha Stevens' vanishing necklace. In my case, there was no drunk involved, and I hadn't even left the restaurant when I noticed it was missing.

Or more precisely, Hetty Green noticed as we were saying our goodbyes. "Georgie, what have you done with that exquisite pearl and diamond pendant? Please tell me you took it off and put it away when you went to the powder room?"

Recalling how startled I had been, even now, I reached for the necklace as I had done last night. As unbelievable as it had seemed, it wasn't there!

Jack and I had done a quick search with

help from the staff who were still around and cleaning up. Our servers had already cleared the dishes and stripped the tables. A waiter shook out the linens that had been tossed into a laundry bin.

The maître d' had called security and a bleary-eyed Adam Drake had shown up minutes into our search. He had taken down the names of all the staff who had been on duty and had gone so far as to frisk the crew members he could round up—including the maître d' who was mortified by the experience. Jack had tried to prevent Adam from doing that.

"No thief skilled enough to get that necklace from you without your noticing it is going to hang onto it," Jack had whispered as we watched from a few feet away. Still, I could understand that Adam was trying to be conscientious.

"He must be following orders from Bill. He wouldn't take it upon himself to do that without authorization from his boss."

"True. Bill must be feeling about as bad as Adam did about this crime spree somehow being their fault. Too much responsibility with too little control—the story of our lives, isn't it?"

"What if it wasn't stolen at all and I flushed it down the toilet or something stupid happened like that?"

"It's all just too much of a coincidence, Georgie. Bold, to pick you out as a target, but it wouldn't be the first time today. You're always quick to blame yourself, too. The sociopaths who choose to become skilled thieves count on the rest of us having all these doubts and desires not to impose upon others or be impolite. I shouldn't be so hard on Adam and Bill."

When we finally gave up and headed back to our cabin, I was close to tears. Jack stopped for a moment and held me in his arms. Lifting my chin, he gazed into my eyes and spoke tenderly but firmly.

"It's just a thing, Georgie. A very pretty thing, true. One that's even more beautiful when you wear it, but it's still a thing. We have so much. All this!" His arm swept wide, drawing attention to our view of the ocean from the deck where we stood wrapped in each other's arms.

The silvery moonlight cast an almost

magical glow upon the water. A breeze rippled, creating a dazzling pattern as though adorning the sea itself in an array of necklaces made of moonbeams and wind. "And we have each other," the kiss that followed made up for a lifetime of lost baubles and more serious misfortunes. I luxuriated as I replayed that moment from last night, but not for long!

"Georgie, my love, are you awake?" I opened my eyes, and three sets stared back at me this morning. My blue-eyed babies sat at the foot of the bed with Jack standing in between them. He held a serving tray.

"How do you do it?" I asked. The cats swarmed me now that I had responded to Jack's question. I was awake—let the feline greetings begin. He must have given them their treats already, or they would not have been so polite.

"Do what?" he asked.

"Wake up refreshed and ready to go no matter what went on the night before! You're up and dressed already—how?"

"Coffee. I have some for you, too. Do you want breakfast in bed or would you prefer to sit out on the veranda?"

"The veranda sounds perfect, although I don't deserve it after losing that pendant!" I replied over the rumbling of my Siamese kitties who took turns greeting me with a head bonk. "No chance it turned up under my seat at The Captain's Table?"

"Sorry, Georgie, there's been no message from the restaurant. We can look around again. The place will be closed until this evening, but I'm sure you can get Gerard to let us in."

"If I can track him down. Where was he last night?"

"You said it yourself that Chef Gerard has his hands full trying to cope with the changes in his luau plans. When Paolo dropped by at the end of the evening, he apologized profusely on Gerard's behalf."

"I know. What a ham—you'd think he was playing a scene from Shakespeare instead of relaying a message form Gerard. I probably shouldn't bother Gerard. He's probably desperately trying to figure out how to cook a kalua pig without access to an imu."

"An imu?" Jack asked, as he headed toward the veranda, then stood there waiting patiently.

"An underground oven you dig in the sand and fill with coals, topped with wet banana leaves to get an authentic smoky, steamed whole kalua pig. That's how Gerard had intended to prepare it for us if we had arrived in Bora Bora yesterday as planned. He had organized this beautiful ceremony with drums and dancers, a procession hauling in that pig with lit torches and chants."

"Wow! I hope word about what they missed doesn't get out and cause a mutiny among the passengers. Some of the chatter last night was less than pleasant." The cats were losing patience, speaking of mutinies in the making. Wave two of head bonks was underway, and I got a sound trampling from them in the process.

"What is it about cats? They're always so excited when their humans wake up, aren't they?" Ella gave me a little pat on the face with a soft paw, while Miles rolled around on the bed. I gave Ella a smooch. She hopped a couple of times and pounced on Miles. He launched himself into the air like Marvelous Marley World's Catmmando Tom superhero. Off they went, racing from our bedroom with the pitter-patter of little cat feet receding into the distance.

"Oh, boy, are they ever wound up!" I exclaimed as I slipped on my robe and opened the sliding doors for Jack. A gust of sea air and a bolt of sunshine hit me all at once. I closed my eyes for a moment, then followed Jack onto the veranda and shut the screen door behind me. Jack set the tray down on the table and poured me a cup of coffee.

"Drink up! I've promised the cats a morning constitutional. Miles is way too smart, by the way. When I said 'leash,' he disappeared in a flash and came back dragging this." Jack pulled a small harness with a leash attached to it from a pocket. A bellow drew our attention to the screen door. Both Miles-the-mighty-mouth and his more mellow companion stared at us.

"So, that's what has them so hyper!" I said as I took a seat at the small bistro table and sipped the coffee Jack had poured.

"Mommy has to drink her coffee first, okay?" I asked Miles who boomed back at me. "That had better be okay because a morning constitutional is not in the cards until the caffeine kicks in, Jack."

Truthfully, coffee is probably a worse addiction for me than chocolate. Somehow, it doesn't leave me with a load of guilt like a chocolate binge. As I savored a sip of coffee, I suddenly realized we were moving.

"Jack, we're underway for Bora Bora. Is there news about Passenger X?"

"Not good news, Georgie. I was hoping you wouldn't ask until after you'd eaten breakfast." He lifted the room service cover from the plate in front of me. "Quiche and fresh fruit. It's delicious," he added, pouring himself a cup of coffee.

"Uh-oh," I muttered as I dug into that quiche. I took a couple of bites and then swigged down the rest of my coffee. "Refill, please." I held my coffee cup near the pitcher Jack had just set down. He obliged. After eating a little more of that quiche and nearly finishing that second cup of coffee, I felt like I could handle the news. I was almost certain I knew what it was, anyway.

"I'm ready. Let me have it. Is it another body?" I asked.

"Yes. The search team recovered a body floating on the water this morning."

"That poor man," I said, hoping more coffee would ease the pounding in my head. "At least now they'll be able to identify him and notify his family of his death." Jack didn't say a word.

"What?" I asked. "There's more?" I flashed on the scene in that cabin last night.

"You might want to hold it a minute before you take another sip of your coffee."

"Is it Abby?" I asked. "Where? How?" I continued pummeling Jack with questions before he could do more than nod yes. I'm not sure why I asked those questions. Far more important than "where" or "how" was "whodunit" and "why."

"He's a she," Jack said. "That man overboard wasn't a man after all."

I should have listened to Jack's warning. I nearly became another victim of the chicanery on board the ship as I tried to swallow without spewing coffee. Once I quit coughing and dabbed the tears from my eyes, I was finally able to speak.

"No way, Jack. The camera caught her on her way to her workout in those cute workout clothes. Wendy Cutler would have noticed. How did Abby end up in nondescript dark clothes not long after the camera caught her in pink?"

"I guess she had a change of clothes in the gym bag she had with her. No wonder she never made it to the spa, and we never got another glimpse of her on video later in the day."

"David Engels showed up too late to get a good look at the passenger falling overboard, but Wendy Cutler couldn't tell it was a woman? At the very least, someone as observant as she seems to be would have spotted that blond hair."

"Unless Abby was wearing a wig."

"What?" I exclaimed.

"Maggie says she has on a wig cap or a wig band or something like that. Her blond hair tucked up under it. She also had one blue eye and one brown one—courtesy of a contact lens that stayed put during that fight and her drowning."

"Drowning? Are you saying she was still alive when she fell into the water?"

"Yes. Probably unconscious, if Maggie's correct in her assessment of Abby's condition. She's only had time to do a preliminary examination of the body."

"A wig and contact lenses have to mean she was in disguise, Jack. Why trade in the perfect cover for pilfering from the spa for drab ware?"

"I don't know. Maybe the thieves were on their way to a theft that required they dress more as stealthy cat burglars. Or Abby decided she liked being on the boys' team better. Given it was so easy to lead them both on, why not join them?"

"But being a girl is what worked for her, Jack. Why give that up? Besides, Abby's the one who was being led on by her teammates for them to have ganged up on her and shoved her overboard."

"Given that Martin Santo took Jake Nugent out, too, I'd say he's the 'player' among the men in that group."

"If she was tossed overboard early yesterday, how did that strand of Abby's hair get caught on the Velcro tab in Perroquet's costume later in the day?"

"If Abby had been in Tina's cabin earlier on this cruise, that hair could have been anywhere in there. We found more of Abby's hair in her cabin last night, too."

"Well, that's odd, too, since stewards had cleaned her cabin before someone ripped that place apart," I said.

"At the time, I just assumed Abby had been in that cabin along with the demolition team. The level of desperation makes more sense if they expected to find something in that room and it wasn't there after they had already killed Abby Kinkaid and Jake Nugent. Who's left to ask about the whereabouts of that necklace or whatever they were trying to find? Even though Abby wasn't there, it's not too surprising strands of her hair turned up. Those hairs could have been in a drawer that was pulled out or on the mattress under the clean sheets. Who knows?"

"What about the blood, Jack? Is that Abby's?"

"It's hard to say at this point since we don't even have a blood type for any of the principle suspects. That's for the FBI agents to figure out, along with all the other unanswered questions about this case."

"Does that mean backup is on the way?"

"Yes, thank goodness! They should arrive in Bora Bora by helicopter when we do in the next hour or so. I'm not sure exactly when they left Tahiti. They could get there before us. Anyway, the sooner, the better. We've done about as much as we can with the resources at our disposal. Both Bill and Maggie have done wonders given the tools available to them and the fact that there are half a dozen investigations underway, not just one."

"Two bodies in the morgue and that loser in the brig ought to make that immediately clear. I doubt even seasoned members of the FBI have encountered that too often on a cruise ship."

"You're right. Hopefully, there are enough clues in all the evidence stored down in the infirmary to nab the culprits, even if they manage to get off this cruise ship when we get back to Papeete tomorrow morning. That's presuming we arrive in Bora Bora, take on the supplies the crew needs, and are underway again this afternoon as Captain Andrews plans."

"I can't get over the fact that our mysterious Passenger X turns out to be Abby. How come she didn't get reported as missing when they did that passenger census?"

"Bill says she wasn't in her cabin when

they made the check, but a woman called in claiming to be Abby Kinkaid. A charge in Abby's name turned up a few minutes later at a coffee shop, too. They used that kind of information to account for passengers who weren't in their cabins."

"Tina could have made that call. Martin Santo must have taken Abby's keycard before he and Jake Nugent shoved her overboard. Clever to use it to make it look like she was still on board. How did he manage to get it from her?"

"We'll have to ask him if we run into him. He's a slippery devil. It's good there aren't as many holes in the hull of this ship as there are in accounting for passengers and crew members. We'd be underwater by now."

"Abby must have turned both men against her if they were willing to work together to get rid of her," I suggested.

"I doubt either man trusted her if they figured out she was playing them both for fools. Romantic triangles sometimes result in bloodshed, but there's even more at stake here. An untrustworthy partner in crime can put you away for a long time. You'd be surprised how many criminal cases get solved because a jilted lover decides to turn in the guilty party, Georgie."

"It still doesn't make sense to me how that leads to murder. I suppose Abby's pals couldn't just punish her by cutting her out of her share of their ill-gotten gains. That could make her more inclined to rat them out."

"It's hard for me to get into their kill-or-be-killed mindset. Abby must have become a liability somehow. Jake Nugent, too."

"Not to mention there are fewer mouths to feed, as you put it earlier. Here's another issue that's bugging me about Martin Santo. Why was he wearing overshoes? If those shoes are standard-issue for members of the kitchen staff, maybe Martin Santo's not a passenger but a crew member. I know Bill says his name doesn't show up on the roster of employees, but that doesn't mean he's not there using another name."

"I'm sure that photo of the man we're calling Martin Santo has already circulated among the crew as well as passengers. I left a message for Bill to see if he can plaster the crew quarters with 'wanted posters' using pictures of all the known culprits. Even though he's done something like that on the electronic bulletin board already, I don't know how often crew members access that site."

"I hear you," I said, disheartened. "If our thieves are in disguise, maybe Martin Santo's face is as big a lie as his name." I wasn't even dressed yet, and it was very early on Day 9 of our honeymoon. Still, I felt a wave of defeat engulf me.

"Georgie, my sweet, I'm a step ahead of you on that one. Heck, we didn't even have the gender right when it came to searching for the missing passenger. I mentioned that to Bill, too, although I'm not sure what to do about it. Maybe he's had a brainstorm since I called him at 6:30 a.m. It's after seven, now."

"Oh, no, are you kidding me? No wonder I feel like I do. You know I don't do early mornings well, Jack."

"Get dressed, Georgie. I'll see if Bill can meet us at The Captain's Table and let us in there to do another search for your pendant. That way you won't have to drag Gerard up there. Bill and I need to touch base about how to manage the handoff to the FBI. We need to speak to Captain Andrews about who's going to provide an update to passengers, now that we're underway. Some of them may have noticed the flurry of activity at dawn."

"It's a good idea to prepare a brief statement, so everyone's on the same page about how to respond to questions from passengers. I can put my PR experience to work and pull something together if that would help." I could hear my phone ping me from the bedroom. I ran to get it.

"Oh no, that can't be Max, can it?" Jack moaned as I hurried to check my messages. "Even he wouldn't contact you before 8 a.m. on your honeymoon, would he?"

"False alarm, Jack. It's not Max," I replied. "Carol texted me. She's going to email me some information," I said as I returned to the veranda.

"Carol? Why? What kind of information?"

"You're not the only one who followed up on some loose ends after we got back to our cabin last night. Since you didn't have anyone who could investigate Paolo's background, I said I was going to ask her to do that, remember? He is a Marvelous Marley World associate, after all. True, in a roundabout way via the cruise line. Carol was more than happy to help when I asked her to check into his background. She didn't even ask for details about why, although she already knew Max was on his way to Tahiti. The word is out—trouble in the South Seas." Jack didn't say a word but wore a skeptical expression.

"Oh, ye of little faith. Look at her message." I handed him the phone as I dashed into the bathroom to shower and dress.

WOWZA! WHAT A HUNK. TOO BAD YOU CAN'T ALWAYS JUDGE A BOOK BY ITS COVER. HIS NAME IS PAOLO VANNELLI—NOT VANNETTI! MORE INFO COMING VIA EMAIL SOON. ONE PICTURE IS WORTH A 1000 WORDS. I'M SENDING SEVERAL.

16 ANAGRAMS AND ARRIVALS

The fresh morning air was invigorating as we strode purposefully up on deck. Well, as purposefully as you can with two cats on leashes. Miles had much more experience on the leash than did little Ella. More than once, I simply had to stoop down and pick her up. Sometimes her curiosity got the better of her, and she refused to move on. Another time or two, the five-month-old kitten became spooked, plopped down and covered her eyes.

"I guess she figures if she can't see scary, it can't see her," Jack said, watching as I picked her up.

"I've been known to do something similar," I retorted.

"Yes, not so different than that old ostrich head-in-the-sand strategy, is it? My parents used that for years trying not to see what they didn't want to see among the less savory members of the Wheeler family."

"That must be especially true with pretty boys like Paolo Vannelli. I can't believe women fall for that hooey he doles out. I hope Carol gets that information to us soon. Maybe there will be enough to upgrade Paolo from a person of interest to a suspect by the time we catch up with the FBI," I said.

"Using an assumed name on his visa and employment application ought to do that for starters—if that's what Carol says he did. That message was a little too cryptic to be taken into evidence. I'll have Bill pick Paolo up and question him once we get that information she's sending you."

"Are we the only two people on board this ship traveling under our real names? What do we pay people in Human Resources to do if they miss something like that with their background checks?"

"It's more complicated when you're trying to gather information from other countries. Many places don't keep records in the same way we do. Some smaller locales don't automate background information. That's still true even in our data-obsessed world back in the states, Georgie. We could try out assumed names if you think that would be fun," Jack raised his eyebrows a time or two.

"No thanks. There's enough confusion about who's who on this fantasy cruise as it is. Oh, Jack, look!" I said as I caught a breathtaking view of our destination. The ragged peaks of Bora Bora were larger now that we were closer to the island. More than a dark silhouette against a brilliant blue sky, they cast an almost mystical vision, as though drawing us to them. Those vivid green craggy points rising from an aqua sea were made more mysterious by a shroud of misty clouds that hung low about them.

"Sights like that make this whole trip worthwhile, despite all the trouble, don't they?"

"They sure do, Jack. If we're only an hour away, that's earlier than Captain Andrews planned to arrive, isn't it?"

"Yes. He was going to wait until more vessels joined us this morning to take over the search. Apparently, Max made that arrangement so the MMW Fantasy of the Sea could move on without abandoning the search altogether, but that's not necessary now," Jack said, sighing deeply.

"That's a good sign that Max is thinking rationally about the loss of a passenger."

"True. Even bordering on the compassionate, although I'm sure your boss is primarily concerned about protecting Marvelous Marley World's image."

"No doubt. Recovering Abby's body puts an end to any misgivings about giving up the search too soon. Another murder at sea and the fact that Passenger X turns out to be an XX and not an XY isn't good news either." Jack looked a little perplexed. "You know what I mean—two X chromosomes as in female rather than an X and a Y as in male...oh, never mind."

"There will need to be clarification about the fact that the man overboard wasn't a man after all. We'll skip the discussion of chromosomes if that's all right with you. The FBI can decide how much to say about the circumstances that make Abby's death a murder." Jack stopped at the entrance to The Captain's Table. He tried the handle, but the door was locked. Then he peered through the window.

"I'm sorry I mentioned it. Good luck explaining any of that in a way that's reassuring to passengers."

"Someone's in there, I think." Jack knocked on the door. No one answered so he pounded louder.

"Hang on, Jack. I've got my keycard," Bill said as he rushed up behind us. Jack was straining to see inside the restaurant.

"I could have sworn I saw movement in there."

"Let's go in and see." Jack and Bill went through the entire restaurant and found no one. Even the kitchen was empty at this hour.

"You two ready for a treat and a nap?" I asked Miles once we were inside. I took his leash from Jack and led the two cats into a corner of the lounge area at the entrance to the restaurant. After a bit of sniffing and a couple of treats, they hopped up next to each other on a plush bench. Like perfect angels, they struck their Sphinx pose and sat perfectly still, side-by-side, staring at Jack and Bill as they began to move chairs away from the table where we had been seated the night before.

Just in case they got the itch to wander,

I looped the end of their leashes around the foot of a heavy Captain's chair near their bench. Then, I went to work, knowing I couldn't count on their perfect angel routine to last for long.

We spent the next half hour searching the empty restaurant for my necklace. Bill had been thoughtful enough to bring latex gloves with him, so I could search the garbage bin in the women's bathroom—just in case it had slipped off in there. Another first and certainly not an activity I had expected to do on my honeymoon.

Once I was satisfied that necklace wasn't anywhere in the lavish restroom, I rejoined the men. They had begun taking items from the side tables and waiters' stations, placing them on the long dining table after examining each object. I followed suit and pitched in. Not long after another wave of defeat had set in, Jack spoke, and Miles let out an ear-splitting call.

"Georgie, come here, please." I rushed to his side. "Do you recognize that?" Jack dumped the contents of a small silver teapot into a gloved hand. My heart sank when I saw what he held. I looked over my shoulder at Miles. *How does he know when something's up?* I wondered. No more Sphinxes. Miles and Ella were sitting straight up like a pair of porcelain figurines.

"That's the clasp from my necklace, Jack, along with a bit of the chain. That clasp is unique and unmistakable."

"A perfect hiding place for a talented thief. I'm almost sure I know who did it and when, too."

"Who?" I asked.

"How?" Bill chimed in seconds later.

"To answer your question first, Georgie. It was the young man who poured our last round of coffee. When you came back from that visit to the restroom, he leaned in and offered to refill your cup, remember?"

"Yes. I know who you mean. I noticed the guy several times—especially when that blowhard was spewing bad puns. Our server tried to hide it, but he was annoyed."

"That's him. As for how, Bill, a touch on Georgie's arm and a flourish with the tea towel draped over his arm must have been enough to distract us as he cut the necklace and slipped it off. I caught him eying you earlier in the evening, Georgie, but what man in that room wouldn't have had his eye on you?"

"Not me, Jack. My necklace, if you're right about him. It's an audacious move to steal my pendant while I'm sitting next to the detective who happens to be investigating murder and thievery on this ship of fools."

"I'm sure that's the point. The bad guys figure they have us outsmarted. With the cruise coming to an end tomorrow, they must have an exit strategy in place."

"Let's round him up, Jack. Adam has the names of everyone on duty last night. If we pull them all together, you can pick him out of a lineup."

"Good luck finding Matt Rosinna, even though his name is on the crew roster. He was long gone by the time Adam started frisking people."

"What makes you say it was Matt Rosinna, Jack?" Bill asked. "There were a dozen names on the list last night in addition to the maître d'."

"The name stands out in my memory now because it's another anagram of Tina Marston—like Martin Santo."

"No!" I exclaimed. "He's a she, too?"

"Like Abby Kinkaid?" Bill inquired a split second later.

Before Jack could reply to either of us, my phone pinged. "It's that info from Carol."

I opened my email message and headed straight for the photos. There was a captioned picture of Paolo Vannelli—not Vannetti—in Vegas, not Tuscany. The newspaper photo showed him standing next to an imposing chocolate castle, holding a blue ribbon, and beaming his Pavarotti-style smile. Behind him and a little off to the side was Tina Marston, or whoever she was, since the caption didn't mention her name. She wore a happy smile, too, along with kitchen whites.

"Aw, what a happy pair," I commented, sarcastically, as I showed that photo to Bill and Jack. It took less than a minute for Jack to explain what Carol had discovered about Paolo's alias. Bill was on the phone in an instant, barking orders to locate and take Paolo into custody.

"I'd say the pretty boy's luck has just run out," Jack muttered, putting an arm around my shoulders. "Let's get out of here. I don't believe there's anything more we can do for now. Once Bill has Paolo in custody, he might need to speak to us again."

A bellow from Miles made it known that he was more than ready to go.

"We're taking the kids home," I said. "You know how to reach us, Bill."

As soon as we were out on the deck, I took a deep breath. While we were inside, searching for my necklace, the ship had reached Pofai Bay. The dark blue color of the deep water where we would anchor stood out in contrast to the lighter color of the shallow water near a startlingly white beach. Beyond, I could see a marina and low-lying buildings that had to be Vaitape. The largest city on Bora Bora, half of the island's ten thousand residents live there. Still, it's a small town by comparison to most any standard.

"I'm a bit sorry we won't be able to explore the island. A lazy swim in the lagoon or snorkeling sounds good, doesn't it?"

"That luau Gerard had planned for last night would have been fun, too. Next time," Jack said as he took my arm.

"Max owes us a 'next time,' after what

we've been through during the past twenty-four hours. What is that sound?" I asked.

"A helicopter—the cavalry has arrived."

"The FBI is landing on the ship?" I asked.

"It would seem so," Jack replied as he stepped close to the rail and shielded his eyes watching as that helicopter hovered. I joined him as the skilled pilot maneuvered onto the helipad. Bill came running from the restaurant, stopped for a moment, and then took off.

"Ari'i nui," he said as he dashed past us. "Tell the Big Chief we've got the bad guy cornered. Someone spotted Paolo down in the commissary kitchen."

"Oh no," I gasped as my stomach did a flip-flop. "It can't be!"

"Speak of the devil," Jack said as we watched the little "Big Chief" step from that helicopter.

17 STOP THAT PIG!

"Is it too late to hide?" I asked.

"I'd say so. For a man in his seventies, his eyesight is excellent. See for yourself."

I moved closer to Jack to get a better view of the 5'6" aged founder of Marvelous Marley World Enterprises. Max sported a white linen suit that set off his white hair. Sure enough, he'd spotted us. Max Marley, now surrounded by several other passengers from the helicopter, was pointing directly at us. Jack and I waved in response.

"Shades of Mark Twain," I huffed.

"At least he's not wearing that little black Colonel Sanders tie like he's on a visit to his old plantation home."

"Given Bill keeps calling him Ari'i nui, I suppose we should be grateful he hasn't shown up in a headdress and loin cloth." Jack burst out laughing as I continued my mini-tirade about Max's sudden arrival.

"Max no doubt took time out for a moment with his fashion consultant, and it's all tastefully done. It strikes me as being rather contrived." I had no sooner finished my sentence than a photographer bounded out in front of that lineup on the helipad and snapped a photo. "Need I say more?"

My phone rang so I couldn't have said more even if I had wanted to keep on griping.

"Hello."

"Ms. Shaw, will you and Detective Wheeler please meet us at the stairs leading to the bridge." Before I could ask who was calling or respond to that request, the caller hung up.

"We've been summoned by Ari'i nui. To the bridge, we must go!" Miles howled in protest. "My sentiments exactly, Miles."

"Maybe you can do that tiki-tiki song and dance in honor of his arrival, and I'll get to hear my new wife sing!"

"I'd rather dive overboard as a sacrifice to the volcano god." That got another laugh from Jack. It only took us a few minutes to get to the bottom of those stairs. As far as I could tell, we were now in Pofai Bay, and the ship had come to a stop.

"What's that?" I asked.

"I think it's one of the ship's tender boats. Maybe it's getting ready to take the landing party ashore for provisions. Max might already be putting the screws to Captain Andrews to get the ship back on schedule as soon as possible."

"We just got here. Early even. There shouldn't be a problem getting back to Tahiti by morning." I shut up at the sound of a calm, stern voice.

"No, Max! That cannot be done." I looked up to see a group huddling above us.

"That is not what I want to hear, Captain. 'Can't' means 'won't' in my book!"

"Then it 'won't' be done, if you'd prefer to hear me say that." Captain Andrews, usually a rational, affable man, was obviously perturbed. "There is no way we can allow passengers to go ashore today and still guarantee our arrival back in Papeete tomorrow morning for disembarkation. We haven't even had a chance to hear what Randall Jennings and his people need from us to assume responsibility for the criminal investigations underway. Passenger safety and restoring security on this ship come before making sure our guests have a good time."

"Please, please, gentlemen. Let's have this discussion somewhere more private," another member of the party suggested.

"Al, I don't need your advice quite yet." Max turned around as he spoke those words. His fists were all balled up. He was moving rapidly into tantrum territory. A breeze had bits of his hair standing on end as though horns were sprouting from his head. His face was already tinged an angry pink.

"Al Hampton is from Marvelous Marley World's law firm. The Board must be concerned about lawsuits from passengers," I whispered to Jack. That's when Max and I made eye contact.

"Georgie! Now here is the voice of reason." Max took two steps down the stairs leading to us.

"This way, please," Captain Andrews said, and the whole party began to follow him. He leaned over from the walkway above us. "Ms. Shaw, Detective Wheeler, uh, uh—all of you, please join us on the bridge." He had stuttered at the sight of the cats with us. Miles was standing, staring back at him in bold defiance of the commotion and bellowed in reply to the Captain's invitation. Little Ella had huddled close and was sitting on my feet.

"Jack and Georgie can fill us in on progress with the investigation, I'm sure. You'll have your answers soon enough about what it's going to take to get matters cleared up, Captain Andrews." Jack shook his head as Max uttered that proclamation.

"Bill Tate and I should confer with the agents from the FBI before I make any pronouncements, Max." Jack nudged me. Ella wasn't going anywhere. I picked her up and started up those stairs. I had the uneasy sensation that I was on my way to the gallows as I took each step. Walking the plank or being hung from the yardarms was a more appropriate analogy for discipline at sea by the unhappy pirate tyrant vying for control of this vessel.

"Where is Bill Tate?" Max asked when Jack and I reached the top of those stairs. Last in line behind Max, we were bringing up the rear in a procession of men in suits and snappy uniforms. *Had that captain's uniform been the inspiration for Max's suit?* I wondered.

"Chasing down a suspect, Max," Jack replied. Max came to an abrupt stop and clapped his hands together. Weirdly elfish, but I preferred the clapping to more of his "pre-tantrum" posturing.

"That is excellent news, Jack. Excellent!" He slapped Jack on the back and then moved forward. He strutted a little as he held his head high and marched after the rest of the entourage.

A half hour later, Jack had briefed the group seated around a gleaming wood table, in a spacious room comprised of windows on three sides. The beauty of our sea view stood in stark contrast to the ugliness of the events that had taken place the past day. Events that ended in the recovery of Abby Kinkaid's body this morning and the identification of two key suspects Bill Tate was currently hunting down.

Mostly, I had remained silent. Except when it came to describing the incidents

Gerard had recounted to me. That included the discoveries he had made in the commissary kitchen, and that "dead duck" message left soon after he began trying to get to the bottom of what was going on.

Jack had asked that they hold questions until the end of our summary of events. By then, we hoped Bill Tate, Adam Drake, and Dr. Maggie Hayward would join us to go over written reports Jack and the other principle participants in the investigation had compiled. When they hadn't shown up by the end of that overview, Captain Andrews had his second mate call Bill Tate on his cell phone.

"Nothing, Sir."

"Try again in a few minutes," Captain Andrews said.

"Will do!"

"If the Security Chief is still down in the commissary kitchen and storage areas, cell phones don't always pick up the signal. Especially now that we're at anchor and may not have repositioned our satellites to optimize onboard communications," Captain Andrews explained to those of us sitting in that room.

Max rolled his eyes and thumped his

fingers on the table. Just as I was trying to figure out what to do next, Maggie walked in. She had a stack of printed material that she distributed. The Captain made a round of introductions as Maggie took a seat a couple of chairs away from me.

"Sorry I'm late, Jack. I wanted to update the reports we had put together with the information collected this morning about Abby Kinkaid. What you have in front of you are written reports about the investigation into Jake Nugent's murder, the disappearance and recovery of Passenger X, who we now know as Abby Kinkaid, and an assault involving Justin Michelson. The bodies of the dead passengers are in the ship's morgue. Justin Michelson is being held below in the brig. There's also a summary of the thefts that have occurred on board during this cruise and an inventory of the evidence that's been collected and stored in a secure location in the infirmary."

We all flipped through the stack of pages in front of us. The amount of material to be covered was daunting. *This review could take the rest of the day,* I thought. *Did Max get that?* He had stopped thrumming his fingers on the table as he scanned the material.

"Where would you like to start?" Jack asked. Before anyone could reply to his question, Miles roared. Ella cried, too. None too politely. The sight of those awful photos made me want to chime in and wail along with them. Instead, I opted to escape.

"I'm so sorry. I need to take the cats back to our suite. Our morning constitutional has turned into a marathon." Jack did not look happy. "If you'll excuse me for 20 minutes or so, I'll drop them off and return as soon as I can. You have lots of material to go through before we can get to the discussion Max wants to have about the ship's itinerary. I'd like to be in on that conversation." I saw Jack's shoulders relax. Murder, mayhem, theft—no problem—facing an imperious, often irrational CEO was another matter.

"Hurry back," he whispered. Max's hearing is as good as his eyesight.

"Yes, do hurry back, Georgie. We have some vital decisions to make. It's almost 10:00 already. Time is not our friend."

"I understand, Max." Since I'd been up and at it since before seven, it felt more like ten o'clock at night than ten a.m. At that point, I raced out of there, especially when I heard

Maggie's opening remarks.

"Shall we start with the preliminary report about timing, manner, and mode of death involving the murder of Jake Nugent? As you can see from photos taken at the crime scene..."

"Let's make our getaway, quick guys!" When we got to the bottom of the steps, I saw that tender boat again. This time it was loaded with people and cargo, including a rectangular container that I recognized immediately.

"How do you like that? Gerard must have gotten permission to take his pig ashore and cook it in an imu on the beach," I said aloud. A man in a tall chef's hat stood on that craft, with a smaller member of the kitchen staff beside him. As I strained to look more closely, I saw two things. The man in the tall hat was a blond, and seated at his feet was Bill Tate.

"That's odd," I said, speaking to the cats again. I pulled out my cell phone and called Gerard. No answer. "Sorry, pals, one quick stop and then we'll go home, okay?" The only reply was a round of chatter—no booming protest.

In two or three minutes, I was at

Kehlani's Lagoon on Deck 2 where the morning buffet was packed. Large dolphin figures wearing flower garlands and leis stood on either side of the entrance. A seating hostess in a colorful Polynesian print shirt and shorts greeted me.

"Oh, what beautiful cats! I wish they could come in and join the fun, but no pets allowed."

"I completely understand, but I have a huge favor to ask. Have you seen Chef Gerard this morning? Is he on the floor of the dining room, by any chance?"

"I haven't seen him this morning at all, now that you ask. He's usually running around, talking to passengers, and making sure the buffet is..."

"I'm sorry to cut you off. It's urgent that I find him. Can you have someone check to see if he might be in the kitchen, please? Tell him it's Georgie Shaw." She must have sensed that my stress level had climbed a few notches after hearing that Gerard wasn't there.

"Sure," she said. "Let me get someone to take my place, and I'll go find Gerard for you." In a flash, a woman dressed in identical garb took her place. She immediately spotted the cats and oohed and aahed at them until hungry passengers arrived, looking for breakfast.

Should I go back and interrupt that meeting? I wondered as I waited for Gerard to join me. What was I going to do, though? Run in there and holler, "Stop that pig!"

I had my phone out and went over the email from Carol, nervously thumbing through those pictures she had sent me. I returned to the one in which Paolo was smiling with Tina nearby. I slid to the next picture in the series and froze. No way! What was going on? I called Gerard on his cell phone again.

"Gerard, it's Georgie. I need to speak to you right away. Call me as soon as you can."

18 A PSYCHO LOGICAL MOVE

"I'm sorry, but no one has seen Gerard all morning. Someone said Paolo mentioned that Chef was sleeping in this morning after a bad night."

"Thanks. Now what?" I asked that question out loud. The young man in kitchen whites stood there staring at me.

"Nice cats."

"Yes, I know. Thanks. Look, uh, Ray," as his name tag indicated, "I need to see Gerard as soon as possible. Can you take me to his cabin? I'm an executive with Marvelous Marley World, see?" He took the I.D. card I handed him and examined it. "I wouldn't impose upon you or disturb him except that it's an emergency. I know my way there, but I don't have access to staff quarters. Do you?"

"Sure, Ms. Shaw. Maybe it'll cheer him up to see you and your cats. Let's go." He returned my I.D. card to me, stepped toward the restaurant, and then realized that wasn't going to work. "This way," Ray said leading me to an elevator designated for shipboard personnel only.

"Does this have anything to do with the guys in that helicopter?" Ray asked as we rode down in the elevator.

"Yes, it does. What have you heard about that?"

"Only that it's about the passenger they found at the crack of dawn. Drowned, right?"

"I'm afraid so. Has anyone said anything to you about changes in the plans for the luau celebration tonight?"

"Since the last change, you mean when it was supposed to happen last night here in port and then it didn't?" The elevator door slid open, and we stepped out into the corridor that led to Gerard's room. He was in the last cabin on this floor.

"Yes, I suppose that's what I mean. It's been a difficult couple of days, hasn't it?"

"You can say that again. No new changes." The cats were straining on their leashes, pulling me forward. Miles let out a low guttural cry that was a cross between a meow and a growl.

"What is it, Miles?" The hair on my arms and the back of my neck stood up.

I reviewed my situation once again as we rushed down the corridor. As far as I could tell, I had three options. One was to call Bill Tate on his cell phone. Until I had a better handle on what was up out there on that tender, that didn't seem like a valid option. If he was a hostage, that call could get him injured or killed. Besides, what if he wasn't a hostage and he was in on whatever was going on? My call could tip him off that he had been discovered making his getaway on that launch. That's why I had decided to try to find Gerard as soon as possible.

My second option was to sound a general alarm with security, but that could have a bunch of unfortunate consequences, too. Like, getting Bill Tate killed if he wasn't on that tender voluntarily, scaring the heck out of passengers, needlessly, or looking like a fool if all of this was paranoia on my part.

A third possibility was to track down the only other guy I knew by name who was intimately familiar with all the trouble on board. Not a high-powered member of the staff, but Bill had trusted him and he ought to be able to tell me what he and Bill had been doing while Jack and I were in that conference room.

"Do you have a way to call security," I asked my companion.

"Yes," he replied.

"Do it, will you, please? Ask for Adam Drake. If you get him on the line, I'd like to speak to him."

Ray looked puzzled as he did as I asked. I heard Ray ask for Adam Drake just as we arrived at the door to Gerard's cabin. I knocked gently on the door. It was closed but not latched. I felt a slight movement as I rapped on the door.

"Gerard," I called out. "It's Georgie. Are you there?" Miles did not wait for an answer. He stood up and leaned against the door, with tiny Ella doing the same. Their weight was sufficient to push open that door wider.

"Gerard!" I cried.

"It's Adam Drake, Ms. Shaw." As I took that phone from Ray, the cats dragged me forward into Gerard's room. Gerard was lying on the floor.

"Adam, it's Georgie Shaw. I'm in Chef Gerard's cabin. Come quickly, but please don't tell anyone where you're going. Hurry," I said as I hung up and handed the phone back to Ray.

The cats were swarming Gerard. When he moaned, I felt a rush of relief. He was alive! There wasn't any blood, either, and no visible sign of injury.

"Ray, can you bring me a damp washcloth from the bathroom, please?" He sprang into action without saying a word.

I knelt on the floor beside Gerard. "Gerard, it's Georgie. Can you speak to me, please? Gerard, what happened?"

"Drugs," was all he said as his eyes fluttered open and then shut again. The cats were tugging at their leashes, straining to reach a coffee cup that lay on the ground. There was a stain on the rug where some of its contents must have spilled when it fell to the floor.

"Oh, no you don't," I said pulling the cats back toward me. Ella went back to bothering Gerard, trying to wake him up. I was about to push her away when she gurgled a sound I recognized as a happy one. Miles was at her side in an instant as we watched her pull my missing necklace from Gerard's shirt pocket. A gasp escaped my lips before I could stop it.

"Here you go," Ray said, thrusting that damp cloth my way. "What's that?"

"Thanks, Ray. That happens to be my necklace. Ella has developed a fondness for it." I probably should have been wearing those latex gloves, but no way was I going to let Klepto-Kitty run off with the evidence. She was a good sport as I took it from her. "Can you hang onto these guys for a second while I see if I can get Chef Gerard to wake up?"

"Wow, when Paolo said Chef had a bad night, he meant it!" Ray took the leashes and backed off with the cats in tow.

"So, true, Ray." I used that cool rag to wash Gerard's face and spoke to him again. If we hadn't searched the restaurant this morning, and put together our own story of how my necklace had vanished, I might have reacted to Ella's find in a much different way. If I had to guess, I'd say Gerard was supposed to have been found in a near stupor with that necklace on his person. Another "patty," as Justin would have said.

"Gerard, I need you to wake up. What was in the coffee? Do you know?" Gerard's eyes opened again. This time he kept them open long enough to see it was me. "Drugs in my coffee, Georgie. Paolo's got the pig." Gerard grabbed hold of me and tried to sit up.

"Hang on, Gerard," I said. "Take it easy." A rush of noise in the corridor made my heart skip a beat. The knock on the door that followed set my heart racing until I heard Adam Drake's voice.

"Georgie, it's me, Adam. I got here as soon as I could."

"Let him in, will you, Ray?" Ray did as he was asked and opened the door.

"Adam, something's happened. Can you help me get Gerard up into a sitting position so he can tell us the whole story?"

In another minute, we had Gerard upright and leaning against the edge of the couch in his sitting room. He sipped water holding the cup in shaky hands.

"Where's the pig?" Gerard asked.

"I'm fairly sure it's in the tender on its way to shore. Paolo, Bill Tate, and another member of the kitchen staff are with it."

"You've got to stop them, Georgie. The stolen jewelry is inside it. They had it in my safe—the one I told you about where I keep the expensive items we use during the cruise. Paolo came for his secret stash this morning. He had a crew member with him. Paolo calls him Marty."

"Was it Martin Santo, Gerard?" I glanced at Adam who nodded as though he understood who I was asking about and why.

"Yes, that's him. He works in the kitchen but picks up a few shifts in housekeeping, too. Now I understand why he was always hanging around Paolo and why Paolo covered for him when the guy showed up late or missed a shift." Gerard drank more of the water from that cup. "I figured they had something going, Georgie— something personal."

"Adam, when was the last time you saw Bill?"

"He had Paolo Vannelli in custody after locating him in the commissary kitchen."

"Vannetti," Gerard corrected Adam.

"No, Gerard, it's Vannelli," I showed him that photo on my phone.

"How is that possible? When was he in Vegas? That wasn't even on his resume."

"I'm betting he had good reason to hide that part of his life from you. Right now, I need to sort things out a bit so we can stop that pig. How do you know the jewelry is in the pig?"

"Paolo laughed about it. He made me sign a requisition asking for the use of the tender to go ashore with that pig so it could be cooked someplace I never heard of before. The order said Paolo and his assistant were going along to ensure proper cooking and handling of the product."

"Bill Tate would never have allowed Paolo Vannelli to do that," Adam remarked. "We had picked him up for questioning as a suspect in the thefts and murders on board this ship!"

"Whoa," Ray murmured from behind us, as he backed up and sank into a chair.

"So, Gerard, Bill had Paolo in custody. Then what happened?"

"Paolo was squawking that he'd injured himself in the scramble to cuff him. Bill agreed to stop by the infirmary so Maggie could check him out. I haven't heard from Bill since then. With the arrival of the FBI by helicopter…"

"FBI? No way!" Ray muttered before Adam could finish his sentence.

"I figured Bill was tied up, filling in the agents and transferring authority to them."

"He may be tied up all right," I muttered. "I'm going to call my husband, Detective Wheeler, and try to explain all this to him. I figured Paolo had to have help from someone with authority on board. I had to be sure that it wasn't Bill."

"I'll get Gerard some more water. Should I call Maggie and have her come check on Gerard?"

"No!" I said more loudly than I meant to do. "She's busy with Captain Andrews and the FBI team doing what you thought Bill was doing."

I placed a call to Jack. "Dang, it!" I said a few seconds later when the call didn't go through.

"Can you get a call through to Jack Wheeler on your phone, Adam?" He gave it a try.

"No, there must be something blocking our reception down here. We should have better luck up on deck."

"Gerard, sit tight. Ray, you're in charge until we get back with more help. Shut the door behind us and don't let anyone in here unless you're certain it's us. Got it?"

"Murder, thefts, drownings, FBI—don't worry. I've got it."

"Come here, Baby," Gerard said. Ella was in that 'can't-see-scary, scary-can't-see-me' position again. I picked her up, gave her a smooch, and placed her in Gerard's arms.

"Mama will be back soon."

Adam and I were on the upper deck in two minutes. My phone still didn't work. Adam had no luck, either. I could see that tender was much closer to shore now. The whole episode locating and reviving Gerard hadn't taken more than fifteen minutes. Still, we had no time to lose. I took off running with Adam at my side. When we got to the foot of those steps leading up to the bridge, I stopped and composed myself.

"Are you authorized to take us up there, Adam?"

"Yes."

"Once you get me through security, I want you to get out of sight. Maggie's in that room. I don't want her to get away."

"Maggie?" It was as if an electric shock shot through Adam. The light bulb came on, and he nodded.

"She's cool as a cucumber, but I doubt she'll stay that way if she sees you with me. It also wouldn't surprise me if she's armed in some way, just in case her plans to keep everyone busy in that room long enough to get the loot ashore came undone. She must be expecting to get a signal of some kind once Paolo's on shore and in the clear. Then I guess she'll excuse herself from that meeting. If that happens, you and your security chums grab her, okay?"

"We won't let her get away. What are you going to do?"

"I'm going to try to play mental telepathy with my husband of a week or so and see if we can't stop this before that tender reaches the shore." I'd try to use a little more than thoughts to get my message across. I composed a short message and texted Jack. That whooshing sound made my heart sing.

I kept that message open on my phone again just in case he didn't get it or read it. Plan B was to sit next to him and pretend to show the proud papa baby pictures of his happy cats.

MAGGIE'S BAD NEWS. MAYBE ARMED. BILL TATE HOSTAGE ON TENDER NEARING SHORE. JEWELS IN PIG. IDEAS?

"Hi, I'm back!" I said in a cheery voice. "Please go on with your conversation. I'll just listen in until I catch up." Maggie smiled, but by the wariness in her eyes, I'd say her antennae were up. I smiled back at her and walked to my seat, trying my best to do as I told Adam I intended to do—read my husband's mind. His phone was out on the conference table, face down. Had he received that message and read it? There was no way to know for sure by his expression or demeanor.

"Baby pictures," I said as I sat down, handing my phone to Jack. He said nothing but smiled as though happy with what he was seeing. I breathed a bit easier, knowing that if he hadn't already done so, Jack was working on the problem now. That's when Max threw a monkey wrench into the entire process.

"Baby pictures?" he asked, just as Maggie seemed like she was about to start speaking again. "We've been looking at horrid pictures. Show us something pleasant, Georgie."

"Yes, why not? Let's take a moment to stretch. You all have been going at this for nearly an hour," Maggie said. Agent Jennings and his partner from the FBI looked askance. Jack stood and stretched, then took my phone straight to them, and shared that photo. An almost imperceptible jolt ran through them.

"What a cute child," Jennings commented. Monkey wrench number two flew from Max.

"Child? What are you saying? I thought you were talking about the cats. Let me see that!" He reached for that phone, and almost had it in his grasp when Jack let it fall.

"Oops," he said.

I glanced out of the corner of my eye, trying to discern Maggie's next move. She bent down as if to scratch her leg. I saw her palm something and caught a flash of metal as she stood.

"Max," she said. As he moved toward her, I panicked. The chairs around that table were on wheels. Before Max could make a move, I shoved the chair next to the one in which I was sitting, hard, using both feet. That sent it careening into the one next to her. That one slammed into her, and her body bent sideways. I hoped she would fall, but no luck.

As Maggie regained her footing, she turned toward me with the most vengeful look on her face I had ever seen. Wielding a small knife above her head, she lunged in my direction.

Max was the closest person to her. His fists balled up and his face turned the scary purplish color that signaled he was in full-blown tantrum mode. His eyes bulged, and spit flew as he screeched.

"How dare you!" Hurling himself after her, he launched himself like a rodeo cowboy onto the back of a bronco. She shrieked and bucked him off. As he fell, he grabbed her by the hair and yanked her backward. All the other men in the room flew into action as Maggie stumbled again but still did not fall. Captain Andrews shouted above the noise.

"Stop right where you are, or I will shoot you." Maggie instantly transformed from raging Valkyrie into a simpering Gollum.

"Please, please, don't shoot," she pleaded as the scalpel in her hand dropped to the floor. Her head down and hands up, tears flowed. Adam Drake came bounding into the room.

"I know you said to wait, but I heard shouting."

"It's okay, Adam. Maggie's disarmed." I said. "Who brings a knife to a gunfight?" I asked as I stared at the guns in the room pointed at Maggie. Jennings and his partner were armed, as was Captain Andrews and his second mate.

"Someone with a *'psycho'* logical problem," Jack retorted. "Do we have anyone who can meet and greet a party heading by tender to Bora Bora? Georgie tells me Bill Tate's on board, possibly in a compromised situation." All eyes turned to me as Jack shared that information.

"I know this is hard to believe, but Paolo Vannelli and a coworker, Martin Santo, have absconded with a pig full of stolen jewels. Martin Santo happens to be a she and not a he, by the way. He's on board as a crew member. She's on board as a passenger—Tina Marston. They're on the ship's tender not far from shore. There are other crew members on that launch. I don't know how many or if they're in on the scheme."

"We've got this," Jennings replied, putting his gun away and pulling out a satellite phone. His partner put Maggie in a chair and cuffed her to it. Jack and I spent a few more minutes explaining what we understood so far about the bizarre situations we had encountered on this ship.

It became apparent to me as we spoke that there were still plenty of blanks to be filled in by talking to Paolo, Tina, and Maggie. I would have nominated Paolo as "culprit most likely to sing like a canary," beaming that

Pavarotti smile as he spilled the beans. After seeing Maggie decompensate into a simpering heap before us, she now went to the head of the line. A lot depended on who could pin the murders on whom. As far as Max was concerned, the blanks that bothered me were minor details. Footnotes to a story already written.

"Well done, Georgie. Excellent work, Jack. I knew you two would have this dustup settled in no time." He beamed at the two of us. "Of course, you did have a little help from me this time, didn't you?"

"Yes, you're a man of action," Jack responded.

"A demon on wheels," I added. Mad Max was on the move again, before I got those words out.

"How soon can we get that tender back here? How many others do you have available, Captain? What sort of timetable are we on at this point? Let's order lunch."

"We'll be back," I hollered to a room that was buzzing with sound and motion. "Let's go check on the kids," I said. "No one's going to miss us for a while."

"Too many cooks, crooks, and cops!" Jack took my arm as we slipped out the door. "Now tell me about this business with the pig."

"An interesting new wrinkle in our adventure, isn't it?

19 MAUI BOUND

On the plane to Maui with the cats asleep at our feet, everything was quiet. After the frenetic activity of the past couple of days, it felt almost as if we were motionless, suspended in time and space among the clouds. Once the FBI had freed Bill and taken Paolo and Tina into custody, the rest of the day was spent wrapping up loose ends. Mostly, that effort fell to Jack.

The shock of what had gone on in that meeting room finally reached Max and he straightened up his act, relinquishing his effort to hijack control of the ship and its itinerary. When Max gets down off his high horse, he can be quite resourceful. Gerard was well enough to oversee preparation for the luau, but he had lost a Sous Chef and a kitchen assistant, along with his pig.

Max found another pig and had it delivered to the ship. He also found Gerard another helper in the kitchen—me. So, on my honeymoon cruise, anchored offshore Bora Bora, arguably one of the most romantic destinations on the planet, I suited up in kitchen whites. Max promised to make it up to Jack and me, by suggesting we stay a few extra days at the bungalow he had reserved for us in Maui. To be honest, I felt comforted by carrying out old, familiar cooking tasks, but took Max up on the offer anyway. That turned out to be a very good idea. By the end of the day, I was even sorer than I had been after my tango with Perroquet. Max owed me those extra days.

My discomfort was worth it. The luau was delightful. Spirits were high as Bora Bora came to us. A swarm of canoes surrounded the ship. Singers and dancers in traditional dress boarded the ship. They were loaded down with flower leis and gifts from the islands. The spirit of Polynesian hospitality on their lips and in their smiles, they sang their goodbyes hours later as their canoes returned to shore set against a blazing sunset.

This morning Jack and I lounged as long as we dared before packing. Then it was a scramble to disembark and catch our flight for Maui. We had exchanged a few updates, but had not spent much time processing the misery that had occurred on board. All that had gone on in the last couple of days seemed inconceivable as I considered it again in the womblike calm of the seats Max had arranged for us in First Class.

The calm _after_ the storm, I ruminated. A storm at sea, courtesy of lost souls, bent on destroying each other—over a bauble. I drifted back to that moment when Jack had spoken with such wisdom about my lost pendant: "It's only a thing." So true. Then again, it is, and it isn't. The shiny things we love so often become symbols of the more intangible objects of our desire—love, safety, security, esteem, and escape from the drudgery and uncertainty of everyday life. *How many lose their lives,* I wonder, *searching for the intangible in the tangible?* I reached out and covered Jack's hand, lying on the armrest between us.

"Why do you suppose Maggie didn't just flee from that meeting?" I asked.

"Where could she go once the jig was

up? She was well past thinking clearly about anything by that point. The discovery of Abby's body and the imminent arrival of the FBI left her with less room to maneuver or escape. Getting the jewels off the ship along with the evidence she had helped gather and stored with such care might have gone a long way toward covering her tracks if the plan had succeeded. Too bad for her that you spotted that pig."

"Those last two days had to have been spent in a state of desperation. Maggie never showed a bit of that until the very end with that ridiculous effort to attack Max and me."

"Her whacked out 'psycho' logic drove her to take one last crack at leaving more suffering in her wake. Why not make Max or you pay the price even though she'd painted herself into that corner? You can't rely on reason to understand irrational behavior, Georgie. Don't get me wrong. Anyone can stumble across the line into crime through ignorance, by giving into a moment of passion or weakness, or by being misled—like Justin. Willful, deliberate planning to live on the other side of that line is another matter. I see it all the time but don't even try to understand it anymore. My job is to stop it if I can."

"I hear you, Jack. Maggie would have been left to her own devices even if Paolo and Tina had made it to Bora Bora since they had no intention of keeping their rendezvous with her."

"What can you expect from partners committed to a dishonest enterprise? Especially when one of those partners is as disturbed as Tina Marston."

"Martina Vannelli, you mean. I almost feel sorry for Paolo. If what he says is true, he's been bailing her out, literally and figuratively, since their parents died and left them to fend for themselves as teenagers."

"With someone like Paolo, it's hard to know how much of what he says is self-serving or playing for sympathy," Jack cautioned. "He didn't fabricate Tina's police record. She's a compulsive liar with no military service to her credit. 'Monster Marston' was a variation on a name she got working out in the gym hoping she could get a job as a performer with one of the Cirque du Soleil type troupes in Vegas. A charming, scary psychopath, 'Monster Martina' as they called her there was a monster all right. No amount of effort on Paolo's part could change that. He would have been better off to let the justice system deal with her, I'm afraid, and move on to make a life for himself. He's a talented guy."

"True, attractive and likable too, when he isn't overreaching," I said. "That's what Gerard saw in Paolo, I'm sure, and why he was such an advocate for him. Maggie, too, since she and Paolo were a couple during his stint as a pastry chef in Vegas. I suppose, since they kept in touch and he talked her into taking the job with the cruise line, their partnership might still have been about more than business. Well-educated and reasonably good at her job, it's a shame that wasn't enough for her," I said.

"It was way too late to go back to that life once she lost control over the monster on her team," Jack said shaking his head. "I haven't heard the whole story yet, but Dr. Maggie Hayward wasn't squeaky clean when she and Paolo were in Vegas. Physicians are hesitant to turn on their colleagues, so unless she opens up about her past, or Tina decides it's to her advantage to blacken the name of her associates, we might never get a complete picture of what makes Maggie tick."

"Clearly that scalpel Maggie brought with her wasn't the murder weapon," I offered.

"No. I figure that must be long gone—probably overboard as you suggested."

"It sounds like Jake and Abby figured out they were in with a bunch of loose cannons the moment Tina went off-plan and snatched that necklace the first night out. Maggie had gone to all that trouble to have a copy made from photos she took when Marsha Stevens wore it on a previous cruise. Too bad it was such a cheap knockoff," I said.

"Jake was better as a fence than he was as a procurer of that fake. Maggie's ambition is partly to blame. Stealing that necklace was a move up for all of them since it was much more than their usual take on a cruise. Still, if they'd kept to the plan, it wouldn't have had to pass for the real deal for long. Maggie would have made the substitution on the last night of the cruise while Paolo kept Marsha entertained. He would have used drugs like those he gave Gerard on Marsha to ensure she was in no shape to notice the switch until the next day when he and the rest of his thieving pals would have already slipped off the ship."

"I'm not sure their plan would have worked, Jack, even if Tina hadn't gone on that rampage. Hetty Green seems convinced that

Marsha's no pushover for men like Paolo. If Abby and Jake hadn't complained to Maggie about Tina, they might both be alive."

"Maybe, but there was no love lost between any of the members of this pack of wild dogs as Maggie referred to them. Abby had snubbed Jake's advances, repeatedly, so why not help Tina feed her to the fishes? It didn't hurt that one less person meant more to go around for the rest of them."

"Yeah, I know, 'one less mouth to feed.' What goes around comes around, though, doesn't it, Detective?"

"He got his, didn't he?"

"Fast, too. Before Jake could get a moment's satisfaction from sending Abby to her watery grave," I said sadly, trying to understand how one human could do such a thing to another. "That didn't quite work out, either, since Abby didn't remain in that grave. The recovery of her body revealed a lot about their *modus operandi* as you coppers say."

"That's the story behind the story with this gang of thieves. Clever planning that doesn't quite work out because they don't stick with the plan."

"It was a stroke of genius for Abby and Tina to come on board in dual roles—as passengers and crew members. Thanks to Abby's skills as a makeup artist, they were able to pass as men. That gave them much better cover than they would have had as two young, attractive women on the crew. Maggie was something of a mastermind," I said, hating to give her even that much credit.

"Paolo helped, too, with glowing recommendations that got Abby and his sister, Tina, hired a couple of years ago, although he and his sister were both using aliases. With Paolo and Maggie among the professional staff and two team members bunking together in the crew quarters, they had access to the ship covered."

"Not to mention, that as passengers, Abby and Tina could mingle, figure out who on board had jewelry worth stealing, and pick it off in the spa or elsewhere. Most of the time, they could do that without even being noticed using Tina's well-honed pick-pocketing skills. Still, they screwed it up—horrifically," I said.

"Yep, with stupid tussles in the commissary kitchen over some piece of jewelry Tina was convinced Abby had hidden there or in her cabin. The mess they made drew unwanted attention from Gerard. That only got worse when Tina threatened him with that ridiculous duck stunt."

"Sending Justin after us was another huge overreaction by Tina, too. It's amazing how helpful their patsy turned out to be as naïve and silly as he was."

"Justin's not going to get off completely, Georgie, but he'll be in much less trouble than he would have been because of his willingness to cooperate with the FBI."

"Willingness to cooperate!" I exclaimed. "He thinks he's a big shot! He acts like being used as a sucker was the best thing that ever happened to him."

"Whatever he thinks, the best thing that ever happened to Justin was ending up in the brig so soon after his rampage as Perroquet. That kept Tina from getting to him," Jack said making a slashing gesture at his throat.

"Oh, Jack. Stop it. It is some consolation that Justin survived. At least the victims of Tina's murderous rages were her scuzzy companions and not unsuspecting passengers like the targets of their thievery."

"Tina is the weak link in this chain of loosely connected ne'er-do-wells who first met a few years back in Vegas. I don't have the whole story about what went wrong. Tina went too far during some scam they had going and beat the 'mark,' as con artists like to call their victims, so badly he ended up in the hospital. Maggie's the one who suggested they leave the country, visit long lost relatives in Italy, and evade the legal trouble Tina faced. That could have been self-serving if Maggie was already mixed up in their schemes."

"Trashing Abby's cabin was insanely stupid!" I said. "Tina left her blood at the scene."

"Maggie made good use of that situation. She made sure we found that shoe that eventually could have put Tina at the murder scene," Jack said. "That's the one piece of evidence Maggie kept. We found it in her luggage. She must not have had complete confidence that Paolo and Tina would do the right thing when they got to Bora Bora with that pig. Her ace in the hole when it came time to face justice, so she wouldn't get nailed for murder."

"Justice won't bring Jake Nugent or

Abby Kinkaid back," I huffed. "It won't undo the stress passengers experienced even though Max will try to make it up to them with credits toward another cruise."

"Most of the passengers will have their missing jewelry returned to them. And, thanks to another misstep by Tina who imagined she could implicate Gerard by stealing your necklace and planting it on him, you have it back."

"I'm just glad that agent Jennings didn't try to take it into evidence. I might have had to tangle with the law to keep it. I know it's just a thing, Jack, but it's a symbol of the beauty we found even while we were up to our eyeballs in all that sludge."

"That sludge is all but forgotten already, my love. All that I remember is the light in your eyes as you held me in your arms and we gazed at the open sea." Jack added a tinge of Irish brogue as he spoke those words.

"Aw, you do have the gift of gab, husband, and a way of making me feel light as a feather. All my troubles vanquished, I feel like I could dance through life with you at my side."

"You don't need me to make you dance.

Although, you weren't so light on your feet when you sent that chair sailing into Maggie and nearly knocked her down."

"To be precise, I was 'off' my feet, not on them. Maggie was getting ready to put Mad Max down like a dog. I had to stop her!"

"Lucky for Max you did that. I won't soon forget the light in his eyes, either. Mad Dog Max, I say." Jack snarled and woofed. He looked so ridiculous that I hooted with laughter.

Miles bellowed from under the seat in front of us. That container muted his call but not by much. The passengers around us stirred.

"Shh, it's okay Miles," I said. "It truly is okay, isn't it?"

"More than okay and this adventure has only just begun." Jack brushed my cheek with a kiss, and then leaned back, pulling the Panama hat he wore down over his eyes. "You gotta grab your forty winks when you can," he reminded me.

I marveled at how Jack helped me find these tiny islands of tranquility even when my angst-prone nature pushed me toward despair. Is that what love is—a string of small transcendent moments bound together by the ups and downs of ordinary life? If so, I'll take it.

--THE END—

Thanks for reading *Murder at Sea of Passenger X*, Georgie Shaw Cozy Mystery #5.

I hope you enjoyed Georgie's latest mystery! Please, please, please leave a review on Amazon & Goodreads. Thanks a bunch. Don't miss the recipes. Some of Georgie's favorite recipes from the story are included below. YUM!

I also hope you've read Georgie Shaw's other cozy mysteries:

Murder at Catmmando Mountain
http://smarturl.it/georgie1

Love Notes in the Key of Sea
http://mybook.to/lovenotes

All Hallows' Eve Heist
http://mybook.to/halloeve

A Merry Christmas Wedding Mystery
http://mybook.to/cozywed.

A new Georgie Shaw Cozy Mystery will be out later in 2017! Until then, why not try a most excellent cozy mystery adventure with honeymoon sleuths, Kim and Brien, in Corsario Cove? Here's chapter one from *Cowabunga Christmas, Corsario Cove Cozy Mystery #1.* Enjoy!

EXCERPT:
COWABUNGA CHRISTMAS
CHAPTER 1 SURF'S UP!

The sound of pounding surf woke me at the crack of dawn. Why not? We had left the doors to the veranda open. We felt safe in our suite up on the sixth floor and the sound of the waves was pleasant last night. *That wasn't all that was pleasant*, I thought as I slipped out of the oversized bed. That bed was a dream, decked out in soft, silky sheets and a plush comforter in creamy colors mirroring the sea, sand and sun. I grabbed a waffle weave spa robe I had tossed casually on a chair near the bed when we returned from a midnight dip in the hotel pool.

The gated area for club members had been

locked at 10:00 p.m., but no matter. Brien climbed over the fence and then opened the gate from the inside, bowing gallantly as I entered carrying champagne and crystal flutes. The gesture was sweet—a side of Brien that made it almost impossible not to love the guy. Of course, he had just violated several resort rules and probably a law or two. He ought to know, given he's licensed in security and has his 'guard card' as the State of California calls it.

As I slipped the robe on, I padded in my bare feet out onto the lavish balcony that spanned the length of our two-room suite. The sunrise was glorious; molten colors spilling over the rolling waves. The air was cool, as it usually is this time of year on California's Central Coast. I felt warmth creep over me as I tightened the belt on the robe and sank down on a comfy chaise.

My robe had not been tossed casually, but frantically as Brien and I lunged at each other the moment we returned to our room after sneaking that swim. We were giggling and out of breath when we burst into our suite and shut the door behind us. Our leisurely moonlit soak had come to an abrupt ending as we ran for it before hotel security could catch us. The entire evening had been like that—bouncing wildly between deliriously romantic and breathlessly sexy; moonlight and surf vying to set the mood.

Not that unusual, I suppose, for a honeymoon. I looked at the rings on my left hand, almost in disbelief. What had I—what had *we*—done? Me, Kim Reed a married woman—Kim Reed-Williams if I went along with Brien's idea to add the hyphen. A little over a year ago, if asked, I would have described myself as a down-and-out loner. Worse, I had been swimming for my life in murky, shark-infested waters. That all changed when murder and mayhem put the celebrated music producer I worked for in prison. When he had found me on the street years before, I was grateful—that was before I knew what it meant to be 'discovered' by *the* Mr. P.

What I'm grateful for, now, is the chance for a do-over. A fresh start, thanks to my new boss and BFF, Jessica Huntington. Brien owes her a lot, too. That included this deluxe honeymoon. Neither of us could have afforded anything close to a real honeymoon after paying for our small, Christmastime wedding. Jessica Huntington—as in the Huntington

Beach Huntingtons—would gladly have paid for the wedding too.

One of the things I got back, though, when I was liberated from my indentured servitude to a scum bucket, was my pride. So, I set limits on Jessica's largesse even though that's not always easy to do. She's sneaky generous and her lawyer skills give her great persuasive power.

"Yo, Kim, where are you?" my sleepy guy called out from bed. His voice grew louder as he got up and walked closer. "Oh, wow, there you are!"

I looked up to see the buff, blond beach-boy I had married, standing there wearing a grin and a towel. The man is built that's for sure. To be honest, physical attraction accounted for a lot of my initial interest in him.

My attraction had been offset by what I took for immaturity and a lack of smarts. Lots of people see Brien that way. Perhaps it's all that unbridled brawn. I did say he's built! Or it could be the surfer-dude-what-me-worry persona he often hides behind. I was wrong and so are they.

The real Brien, the man I married, is a sweet, guileless guy. A little immature, true, but what 25-year-old man isn't? It could be my California dude is too laid back for most people. Or possibly there's something odd going on in the frontal lobe—a missing filter or switch that should keep him tuned in better to the world around him. Who knows, who cares?

As it turns out, dumb he is not, and he's a hard worker once he makes a commitment. Like working out the disciplined way he does to keep that body of his in such 'righteous' shape, as he would say. There is a simplicity about him that I find appealing. I'm quite sure he'd be content to live in a shack on the beach; workout, surf, listen to music, take in the sunsets with a 'brewski,' and eat, of course. My surfer boy can put it away.

Now, I'd have to add 'hanging with me' to that list of the things that make the light shine in Brien's eyes. Still, a lot comes out of his mouth that he should think about first, or keep to himself altogether. I like him that way—I never need to worry about what he's really thinking. I always know where I stand. At least after I sort out what he means given that he's prone to malapropisms and uses tons of surfer lingo.

Me, I'm not nearly so verbose and can go for long stretches without saying a word. Talk about yin and yang. I'm darkly moody, he's pathologically optimistic and upbeat. I don't trust anyone, he trusts everyone. He's blond and has brown eyes with specks of gold in them. In contrast, my hair is black and my eyes are dark. He's big—not all that tall at about 5'8", but muscled. Me, I'm petite. The differences go on and on. Opposites do attract, so they say.

"Morning, Dude."

"Morning, Gidget," he said, holding onto the smile, but dropping the towel. *Sometimes our moods do match*, I thought as I let him pull me up out of the lounge chair and into his arms. I laughed as he swept me off the floor and carried me back to bed. Who knew what surprises the rest of our day would bring?

~~~~~

Read the rest of *Cowabunga Christmas!* Amazon @ http://smarturl.it/cove1

Gnarly New Year! is out now, too! http://smarturl.it/cove2

RECIPES

Rumaki

24 pieces

INGREDIENTS

1/4 pound chicken livers, trimmed and rinsed
1/4 cup soy sauce
1 tablespoon finely grated peeled fresh ginger
2 tablespoons packed light brown sugar
1 clove fresh garlic
12 canned water chestnuts, drained and halved
horizontally
8 bacon slices (1/2 pound), cut crosswise into
thirds
24 wooden toothpicks

PREPARATION

1) Cut chicken livers into 24 (roughly 1/2-inch)
pieces. Chop garlic fine. Stir together soy sauce,
garlic, ginger, and brown sugar. Add livers and
water chestnuts and toss to coat. Marinate,
covered and chilled, at least 1 hour.
2) While livers marinate, soak toothpicks in
water 1 hour. Drain well.
3) Preheat broiler.
4) Remove livers and chestnuts from marinade
and discard marinade. Place 1 piece of bacon
on a work surface and put 1 piece of liver and 1
chestnut in center. Wrap bacon around a piece

of chicken liver and a chunk of chestnut and secure with a toothpick. Place each rumaki on the rack of a broiler pan.

5) Place about 2 inches from the broiler, turning once, until bacon is crisp and livers are cooked but still slightly pink inside (unwrap 1 to check for doneness), 5 to 6 minutes. Serve immediately.

Georgie's Tips

Rumaki is one of many "pupus"—bite size appetizers—you'll find at Polynesian or Asian restaurants. Pupu platters popped up at tiki-inspired restaurants during the 50s and 60s. You can still find them at many Asian restaurants. If you're planning a backyard or beachside luau, you'll need lots of these little goodies to feed the family and friends who gather.

Luaus don't seem to have originated in Tahiti or the other Society Islands, but in Hawaii. They're found pretty much everywhere in the islands, now, and no ship in Max Marley's fleet that cruises to the South Seas would be without one. Let the feasting begin!

The classic version of rumaki is made with chicken livers. It's the way I first learned to prepare it. Since then, though, I have created rumaki using other delicious tidbits wrapped in bacon alone or in combination. Just leave out the chicken livers and prepare it with the water chestnuts or substitute 24 chunks of fresh

ANNA CELESTE BURKE

pineapple or pitted dates for the chicken livers. The marinade in this recipe gives whatever you wrap in bacon a hint of the exotic, so don't skip it. Try shrimp or scallops, chunks of chicken breast, beef tenderloin, or duck breast instead of the chicken livers. Serve with a small side of Chinese hot mustard, Japanese wasabi, Sriracha, Sambal, sweet chili sauce or your favorite condiment.

Sweet Teriyaki Beef Kabobs

36 pieces

INGREDIENTS

2 pounds beef tenderloin or any lean tender
beef cut into 1-inch cubes
1 (16 ounce) can cut pineapple (reserve juice)
1 tablespoon sesame seeds, toasted
1/4 cup brown sugar
1 garlic cloves, minced
2 scallions, minced
2 teaspoons fresh ginger, minced
1/2 cup soy sauce
1 cup reserved pineapple juice
2 teaspoon cornstarch
1/4 teaspoon pepper

PREPARATION

1) Whisk together the brown sugar, garlic,
green onion, ginger, soy sauce and 3/4 of the
reserved pineapple juice.
2) Toss beef in 2/3 of the mixture and marinate
overnight.
3) Place remaining mixture in a saucepan and
simmer over medium heat.
4) Mix remaining 1/4 cup reserved pineapple
juice with cornstarch and pepper, then add to
the simmering sauce.
5) Reduce to low heat and whisk. Simmer for
10 minutes to thicken sauce.
Strain and reserve. Chill to store, then reheat
when ready to serve.

6) Preheat grill or broiler.

7) Remove beef from marinade and drain well.

8) Soak short 4 or 6-inch bamboo skewers in water for 1 hour.

9) Put 1 beef tenderloin cube and 1 pineapple chunk onto each bamboo skewer.

10) Grill or broil beef skewers about 5 minutes on each side until beef is cooked.

11) Top with additional sauce and sprinkle with toasted sesame seeds.

Georgie's Tips

Teriyaki anything is good, but teriyaki beef is another classic. Don't overcook this dish so that the beef remains tender. The enzymes in the pineapple juice are good to include in a meat marinade because help tenderize the meat.

The teriyaki marinade when combined with cornstarch will thicken it into a sauce. How thick or thin depends on how much of the cornstarch you add.

Try marinating shrimp, chicken, vegetables, or just plain pineapple instead of beef, putting them on skewers under the broiler or on a grill. For your friends who don't eat meat, use cubes of extra-firm tofu instead of beef and make them super happy. On other occasions, you can also use this sauce to create a teriyaki inspired stir fry—adding that pineapple juice & cornstarch at the very end.

Shrimp Toast

INGREDIENTS

1/2 lb shrimp, peeled & deveined
3 tablespoon water chestnuts
1 teaspoon minced ginger root
1 clove garlic
1 teaspoon sesame oil
1 teaspoon cooking sherry
2 teaspoon soy sauce
1 tablespoon slightly beaten egg
1 teaspoon cornstarch
2 scallions finely chopped
1/2 cup sesame seeds
10 slices white bread
24 oz peanut oil or EVO for frying

PREPARATION

1) Cut the crusts off the slices of bread and set out for a few hours to dry out.
2) Pulse shrimp, garlic, water chestnuts, ginger, sesame oil, sherry, soy sauce and egg to a coarse puree.
3) Stir together with cornstarch, scallions and 1/4 teaspoon salt. [Reserve a tablespoon of scallions for garnish]
4) Spread the mixture on the bread and cut each slice into quarters—half squares and half triangles.

5) Pour the sesame seeds on a plate and take one of the quarters and press into the seeds, shrimp paste side down.

6) Repeat for half the squares and half of the triangles, and leave the rest plain.

7) Wrap in plastic and refrigerate until ready to fry.

8) Heat 1-inch depth of oil to very hot, but not smoking. A few bread crumbs dropped in should sizzle right away.

9) Fry the quarters a few at a time by lowering them paste side down into the oil with a slotted spoon for about 1 minute.

10) Flip them over and fry a few more seconds.

11) Drain on paper towels. Garnish with 1T of scallions.

Georgie's Tips

This is another classic pupu. The oil needs to be hot but you don't want it to burn and smoke—use the sizzle test as directed above. These crispy, savory bites are best served immediately, but you may fry them ahead of time and reheat 5 minutes in a 300° F oven, or keep them for a few minutes in a warming oven. They also may be frozen then heated in 325° F oven for 15 minutes.

Pork & Mango Skewers

40 pieces

INGREDIENTS

3/4 cup Hoisin Sauce
3 tablespoon soy sauce
1/4 cup rice wine vinegar
1/4 cup olive oil
1 tablespoon ginger, minced
2 pounds pork, cut into 3/4-inch cubes
3 mangoes, cut into 3/4-inch cubes

PREPARATION

1) Whisk together all ingredients except pork and mangoes.
2) Add pork and mango cubes and marinate overnight, stirring occasionally.
3) Prepare a grill or broiler.
4) Soak 40 short 4 or 6-inch wood skewers in water for 1 hour.
5) Put 2 pork cubes and 1 mango cube on each skewer.
6) Grill or broil for 7 to 8 minutes, turning once.

Georgie's Tips

This is a simple and delicious recipe. Chicken, shrimp, tofu, or beef works well, too, for these mini-kabobs if you don't eat pork. Hoisin sauce is widely available in the Asian food aisle at your grocery. It works well as a substitute for barbeque sauce on just about anything you grill. Just terrific for stir fry dishes, so keep it on hand.

Spicy Coconut Pineapple Shrimp Skewers

30-40 pieces

INGREDIENTS

1/2 cup light coconut milk
4 teaspoons Tabasco or your favorite hot sauce [use less if your choice is a very hot, hot sauce!]
2 teaspoons soy sauce
1/4 cup freshly squeezed orange juice
1/4 cup freshly squeezed lime juice (from about 2 large limes)
1 pound large (31-40 count) shrimp, peeled and deveined (you can use fresh or frozen, thawed shrimp)
3/4 pound 1 inch-cut pineapple chunks
Olive or canola oil, for grilling
Freshly chopped mint and/or green onion and shredded coconut for garnish

PREPARATION

In a medium bowl, combine the coconut milk, hot sauce, soy sauce, orange juice, and lime juice. Add the shrimp and toss to coat. Cover and place in the refrigerator to marinate for 1-2 hours, tossing occasionally.

Soak small [4 or 6-inch] wooden skewers in warm water while the shrimp marinates. Cut fresh pineapple into chunks [sometimes you can find them at your grocery already cut into chunks].

Preheat the grill to medium high heat—375-400 degrees F. Remove the shrimp from the marinade, and reserve the marinade for grilling. Slide a chunk of pineapple, a shrimp, and then another piece of pineapple onto each of the wooden skewers.

Lightly brush the grill with oil, then place the skewers on the grill. Grill the shrimp for 3 minutes, brushing with the marinade, then turn and cook for an additional 2-3 minutes, brushing with the marinade again, until the shrimp are just cooked through. Remove to a serving plate and garnish with mint, green onion, and shredded coconut. Serve hot.

Georgie's Tips

Cooking shrimp always requires care not to overcook. These are wonderful on the grill, but in a pinch a broiler will do. Leave the hot sauce out of the marinade if you don't like spicy. Serve these with a side of sweet chili sauce instead.

Using full-size skewers, these appetizers can become a great dinner entree when served over rice. Add chunks of red pepper, white onions, cherry tomatoes, or mushrooms into the mix if you like. Healthy and delicious!

Kalua Pork*
Serves 8-12

INGREDIENTS

4 c mesquite wood chips
4 lb pork shoulder
1 ½ teaspoon Hawaiian Pink Sea Salt
Banana leaves

PREPARATION

1) Place the wood chips in a bowl and cover them with water. Let them soak for 1 hour, at least.

2) Prepare your smoker or grill as you normally would with coals. Preheat your smoker to 200-250 F (or set your grill for indirect cooking at 200-250 F).

3) Rub the sea salt into the pork and wrap it in banana leaves. Tie the leaves with kitchen twine, so the packet stays together.

4) Add a couple of handfuls of soaked mesquite chips to the hot coals in your smoker and place a tray of water under your cooking grate.

5) Smoke your roast between 200-250F for 8-10 hours, adding wood chips and charcoal every hour to keep it going.

6) The meat is done when it has reached an internal temperature of 160F. Remove the meat from the smoker and let it stand for 10 minutes before unwrapping and serving.

Georgie's Tips

Kalua means 'the pit' in Hawaiian, referring to the traditional method of cooking. Short of digging a pit in your back yard and creating your own imu, this about as close as you're going to get to the real kalua pig [no need for a whole pig, either, like at a luau!]

Where do you find Hawaiian sea salt and banana leaves? Believe it or not, Walmart sells them online if you can't find them at a local Asian or Latino grocery. Serve with steamed rice and a cabbage slaw or macaroni salad and Hawaiian sweet rolls to reproduce the Hawaiian "plate lunch" experience.

What do you do if the fire goes out on you after a few hours? It happens, I know! Finish the pork in an oven set at 200-250 degrees.

Don't have a grill or a smoker? There are several recipes available that suggest you steam the pork shoulder in a crock pot and use liquid hickory or mesquite smoke instead of slaving over hot coals to produce this dish. This method still requires a lengthy cooking time but you can leave it and go do other things: http://www.familyfreshmeals.com/2016/07/3-ingredient-crockpot-kalua-pork.html

If you want to try a slow cooker version of kalua pork and don't want to use liquid smoke, here's a link to a recipe that uses bacon to give

the pork roast a smoky flavor instead:
http://nomnompaleo.com/post/10031990774/
slow-cooker-kalua-pig. Simmer cabbage in
some of the juices from the pork for a great
side-dish.

Sam Choy has an oven roasted version that
uses banana leaves and liquid smoke. You can
find his recipe at:
http://www.epicurious.com/recipes/food/view
s/sam-choys-oven-roasted-kalua-pig-233927

If this Polynesian twist on the southern
tradition of "pulled pork" grabs you, try several
versions and see which one you prefer. Kalua
pork is great with rice, beans, or cooked greens.
Try it in your favorite Mexican dishes. It's great
in quesadillas, on nachos, or in tacos or
burritos.

*Based on a version of the recipe found here:
https://www.curiouscuisiniere.com/kalua-pork/ You'll
find some pictures, too, about how to tie up the pork in
those banana leaves.

Duck Magret with Fig & Port Sauce

Serves 4

INGREDIENTS

4 boneless Magret or regular duck breasts
(about 8 oz each)
2 tablespoon minced fresh thyme
¾ teaspoon each salt and fresh ground pepper
1 shallot, minced
¾ cup port wine
1 tablespoon balsamic or fig vinegar
8 dried figs [black mission or Turkish],
quartered [plus 2 fresh figs for garnish if you
can find them at the grocery store]

PREPARATION

1) While the duck breasts are still cold from the refrigerator and the fat is firm, score them through the skin and fat, but do not cut into the meat. Make the scores on an angle about 3/4" apart. Let the duck breasts sit and come to room temperature so they are not cold when you start to cook them (30-45 minutes). Just before cooking sprinkle with half of the thyme, salt and pepper.

2) Heat a large heavy skillet over high heat. When hot, place duck breast into pan, skin side down. Reduce heat to medium. Cook slowly

until duck is a rich, golden brown, about 8-10 minutes. Turn and cook until seared on second side about 3-5 minutes. You want to serve these duck breasts medium rare. Place a thermometer in the center of the thickest part of the meat and stop cooking when you get a reading of 135-140 degrees F.

3) Transfer duck, skin side up, to a plate—tent with tin foil. Drain fat from pan, returning 1 Tbsp. to pan. **Fry shallot and remaining thyme until shallot is translucent, about 2 minutes.**

4) Combine port, vinegar, figs, salt, and pepper and heat over medium-high heat. Bring to a low simmer, stirring occasionally for about 3-5 minutes. It should thicken a little.

5) Place duck breast on a cutting board and slice each breast diagonally into thin [1/2 inch] slices. It should be served medium rare and will be pink inside.

6) Divide duck slices among four plates. Spoon sauce and figs over and around duck. Quarter the fresh figs and garnish each plate. Add sides of mashed potatoes, steamed vegetables, and warm, crusty bread or rolls. Serve immediately.

Georgie's Tips

Magret refers to the type of duck breast that's used in this recipe. Large and meaty like a steak, they cost a little more and are usually found in specialty stores or online. You can use regular duck breasts [usually from White Pekin ducks], but you will want to reduce the cooking time and make sure they don't dry out.

How do you "tent" the duck to keep it warm? Tear off a piece of aluminum foil large enough to fit loosely over the plate you're using for the duck. Place the foil shiny side down, loosely, over the duck so it reflects the heat back down over the food.

You're likely to have a lot of duck fat left in the pan once you have finished cooking the duck breasts. Many chefs save the rendered duck fat to use later. Try drizzling a tablespoon of duck fat [instead of olive oil] when roasting potatoes or other vegetables. There may even be some health benefits to using this form of fat for cooking.

Once you master the cooking process for duck breasts, you can create amazing dishes using other sauces—like a caramel blueberry sauce, citrus or herb butter, or spiced cherries. Yum! Duck loves fruit so there are lots of options out there for you.

Quiche Lorraine*

Serves 6

Ingredients

1 8 or 9-inch pie shell, frozen [see recipe to
make your own pa brisee—pie dough—below]
8 bacon slices
2 shallots
3 eggs
1½ cups cream or half-and-half
½ teaspoon salt
pinch of freshly ground pepper
pinch of nutmeg

Preparation

Preheat oven to 400 degrees. Line the pie crust
with aluminum foil or parchment paper and fill
with dried beans or pie weights. Bake in the
preheated oven for 8 to 9 minutes. Then
remove the foil and pie weights and cook for 2
or 3 minutes more, until the shell is starting to
color. Remove from the oven and reduce the
oven temperature to 375 degrees F.

Meanwhile, prepare the filling. Over medium
heat, cook the sliced bacon in a skillet until
crisp. Remove and place on a plate lined with
paper towels to drain. Remove all but a
tablespoon of the bacon fat from the pan. Then
chop the two shallots and sauté them in the
bacon fat until they soften, about 2 minutes.

Once cooled slightly, chop bacon. Scatter shallots and bacon evenly over the bottom of the partially-baked pastry shell. Next, beat the cream (and/or half-and-half) with the eggs, salt, pepper, and nutmeg, until well blended. Pour over the chopped bacon and shallots. Bake in a 375-degree oven for 30-40 minutes, until the quiche has puffed up and browned. Serve warm or cold.

*This recipe is a variation on Julia Child's classic! http://www.wgbh.org/articles/Recipe-Quiche-Lorraine-7087

Georgie's Tips

Use a light-colored pie tin or tart pan to prevent over browning. You can also you can use a crust shield to prevent your crust from becoming too brown.

The key to a great quiche is getting the right mix of dairy & eggs! Use 1/2 cup dairy for each large egg. A 3-egg quiche, like this one, has 1 1/2 cups of milk or cream or half and half.

And then there's the cheese...for a 3-egg quiche, 1 cup of cheese will keep this light but give it depth, too. Vary the amount to your taste, though.

In fact, once you have this basic quiche idea down, experiment! Try removing the bacon and add fresh mushrooms or spinach instead. That give you a lovely vegetarian main dish. Switch out the gruyere for cheddar and you have an eggs, bacon, and cheese combo that's perfect for breakfast. Don't add anything that will dilute the egg & cream mixture, so, for example, use fresh mushrooms or drain canned ones well, first. This is an amazingly versatile dish that can accommodate your favorite vegetables, like asparagus or broccoli. Add bits of ham, sausage, or chicken instead of bacon.

You want your quiche to have a firm, custard-like quality, but don't overcook. Use a thermometer the first time out. Place it in the middle of the quiche—not touching the pan—and take it out of the oven when it reaches 170 degrees.

Serve with a crisp green salad and fresh fruit as a delicious lunch or light dinner. If you drink wine, a chilled Chardonnay or another white wine would go well with your quiche.

Pâte Brisée
8 or 9-inch pie/tart shell

INGREDIENTS

1 1/4 cups all-purpose flour
1/2 teaspoon salt
1 teaspoon granulated white sugar
6 tablespoons [3/4 cup] unsalted butter,
chilled, and cut into small pieces
1 large egg
Small amount of ice water [no ice]

PREPARATION

Place the flour, salt, and sugar into a food
processor and pulse until well combined. Add
half of the butter cubes and pulse 6 to 8 times.
Then add the other half of the butter cubes and
pulse 6 to 8 more times. You should have a
mixture that resembles a coarse meal.

Add the egg and pour it into the bowl in 3 small
additions, mixing for a few seconds each time.
(Don't overdo it or the dough can get tough).
You'll have a moist, pliable dough that will hold
together when pinched. If that doesn't happen,
add a tiny splash of ice water [start with 1
teaspoon] and pulse again.

Turn the dough out onto a work surface, gather
it into a ball (if the dough doesn't come
together easily, push it, a few clumps at a time,

under the heel of your hand or knead it lightly). Flatten it, slightly, into a disk.

Wrap the disc in plastic wrap and refrigerate at least 1 hour. [NOTE: All of this can be done a day or two ahead. The dough can be frozen and stored even longer. So, double the recipe, make 2, put one in the fridge and one in the freezer for later.]

When you are ready to roll out the dough, remove from the refrigerator and place on a clean, smooth, lightly floured surface. Let it sit for 5 to 10 minutes so that it becomes easier to roll out.

Roll out the pie dough into a 12-inch round. Wrap it around the rolling pin, lift it and place it in a 9-inch pie plate, gently pressing the dough into the pan. Use a rolling pin to roll over the surface of the tart pan to cleanly cut off the excess dough from the edges. Here's a YouTube Video demonstrating this process: https://www.youtube.com/watch?v=QxMAQY Ro5t8

Or cut away the excess with a knife if you're using a pie pan, leaving enough to crimp the edges if you'd like. Freeze for at least half an hour before blind-baking if you need a partially-baked or pre-baked crust. By that I mean, line the chilled dough with parchment paper or foil. Fill the inside with pie weights or beans and bake until the edges of the crust begin to brown. Remove the pie weights before filling the crust. See my note below, though!

Georgie's Notes

This recipe is like a traditional pie dough recipe except that there's no lard, and you add an egg. I confess I'm intimidated by making my own pie dough and often resort to using the ready-made ones you can find in grocery store freezer sections. Trader Joe stores out here in California have great ones that are so tasty they make me even less inclined to make dough from scratch. If you have a favorite already, stick with that. Clarks, a local health food store, even has frozen premade GLUTEN FREE crusts!

Those aren't quite the same when it comes to making savory tarts, though. I think this recipe is easier to work with than traditional pie dough recipes. So, if you have the time, why not try making *pâte* brisée from scratch?

Okay, so blind bake or no? I've had good luck cooking the pie dough without the parchment paper weights just by pricking the bottom with a fork. That seems to be true if, after rolling out the dough and placing it in the pan, I freeze it to set it for 15-30 minutes before baking.

Chocolate Ganache Tart
Serves 8

INGREDIENTS

Pâte sablée Crust:
1 1/4 cup all-purpose flour
1/8 teaspoon salt
½ cup unsalted butter, room temperature
1/3 cup confectioner's sugar
½ teaspoon vanilla or 1 vanilla bean, halved, seeds scraped
1 large egg yolk, separated
1 tablespoon cream or milk [if needed]

Chocolate Ganache Filling:
8 ounces bittersweet chocolate, finely chopped
4 ounces semisweet chocolate, finely chopped
4 tablespoons unsalted butter (1/2 stick), cut into small pieces
1 cup heavy cream
3 tablespoons granulated sugar
1/4 teaspoon fine salt

PREPARATION

CRUST

In a mixing bowl, cream softened butter together with powdered sugar; add in egg yolk and vanilla, then mix until incorporated; add in the flour and be sure to only mix until the last trace of flour begins to disappear. If the dough appears dry or doesn't hold together at this point, lightly mix in up to 1 tablespoon cream or milk.

Prepare a 9-inch tart pan with a removable bottom, lightly buttered and floured. Sprinkle dough evenly over the bottom. Using your fingers, press the dough into the bottom and up the sides of the pan. Dip your fingers in flour if the dough starts to stick to them.

Preheat the oven to 375°F. Wrap the pan loosely in plastic and freeze for 15 minutes. This sets the crust so it won't puff up while baking. Also, gently prick the bottom of the crust before baking which also prevents the pastry from puffing up [See my notes about "blind bake or no?" if you have questions about using this baking method]. Bake until golden brown, about 25-30 minutes.

FILLING

Place chocolate and butter in a medium bowl; set aside.
Combine cream, sugar, and salt in a small saucepan over medium heat and stir until sugar dissolves and liquid is just at a simmer, about 4 minutes.
Pour cream mixture over chocolate and butter and let sit until melted, about 4 minutes. Gently stir until smooth.
Pour ganache into the cooled tart shell and transfer to the refrigerator. Chill 2-3 hours.

Georgie's Tips

Unlike a flaky pie crust, pâte sablée is crisp and crumbly. The name literally means "sandy," although it's more cookie-crumble good than anything you'd call sandy. Pâte sablée is a classic French shortcrust pastry dough that, once baked, becomes the base for any tart you can imagine.

Pâte sablée is a very manageable and approachable kind of dough—easier and more forgiving than other pastry doughs. I'm much less intimidated and love making this dough from scratch. Other than a bit of resting time between steps, it is a relatively simple and straightforward recipe. You can make the dough ahead and keep it refrigerated for a day or two.

When using pâte sablée, the crust needs to be either partially or fully baked before filling. The rule of thumb is that the less time the filling needs to bake, the longer the crust needs to bake on its own. So, in the cases where the filling needs just a little baking, like with frangipane, the crust should be partially baked. If the filling does not need to cook at all (like for pastry cream, whipped cream, fresh fruit, etc.), then the crust needs to be fully baked.

Most recipes for tarts using this dough will recommend that you "blind-bake" the tart for about 20 minutes. In other words, line the chilled dough with parchment paper or foil. Fill the inside with pie weights or beans and bake until the edges of the crust begin to brown. Remove the pie weights. Then return the crust to the oven and bake another 5 or 10 minutes until entire crust is a golden brown. Try "setting" the pâte sablée dough by freezing for 15-30 minutes in that tart pan or pie tin first. Then bake it as you need to do for your tart by simply pricking the bottom with a fork instead of using the blind-baking strategy. Do this when you're rehearsing the tart you plan to make for a special event, though, to see if it works for you!

Ganache is a fancy word for what is basically chocolate [yum!] with warm cream poured over it. Let it melt the chocolate on its own, then mix. If you stir too much too soon the mixture can get grainy. Use it as a glaze over candy, cake, or brownies or as a filling between cake layers. Let the ganache cool so that it will spread more easily over cake layers. For more variety, you can add other flavors to this chocolate ganache. Check this site out for ideas:

http://www.easy-cake-ideas.com/chocolate-ganache.html

Whoa, wait! What about the Bavarian cream and Passion fruit syrup on that chocolate tart I described in Murder at Sea of Passenger X? That takes a bit more work but here's how to do it. You need a Bavarian cream and a passion fruit syrup. Here goes!

Make a Bavarian cream to add as a layer over the ganache...

<u>Bavarian Cream Ingredients</u>
1 Tahitian Vanilla bean, halved, seeds scraped or ½ teaspoon vanilla extract
1 1/4 cups heavy cream
1 tablespoon powdered gelatin
3 tablespoons milk
1/4 cup sugar
5 egg yolks
1 1/4 cups whipped cream

<u>Bavarian Cream Preparation</u>
Put the split vanilla bean in cream and slowly bring to a boil. Turn off heat and let sit for 1 hour. Remove bean and scrape out seeds, add them to the cream and discard the pod. [If you use vanilla extract instead of the vanilla bean, scald the milk as above but wait until it's cool to add the vanilla extract]. Sprinkle the gelatin into the milk and set aside.

Whisk the sugar and egg yolks together. Warm the cream mixture back up and slowly whisk into eggs. Place mixture over simmering water and stir until it is thick enough to coat the back of a wooded spoon. Remove from heat and add milk and gelatin mixture.

Place bowl in an ice bath and stir until it reaches room temperature. Fold in whipped cream and spread a thin layer of Bavarian cream over the top of the cooled ganache tart. Return to fridge and chill for at least an hour or until you're ready to serve it. If you have Bavarian cream leftover, use it on top of French toast or pancakes, as a filling for crepes or blintz, or all alone as a rich pudding.

Drizzle with passion fruit syrup. While the tart is chilling, or ahead of time, make the passion fruit syrup...

Passion Fruit Syrup Ingredients
1 cup water
1 cup sugar
1/2 cup passion fruit pulp (from about 7 ripe passion fruits), strained to remove seeds

Passion Fruit Syrup Preparation
Combine all ingredients in heavy small saucepan. Bring to boil over medium-high heat, stirring until sugar dissolves. Reduce heat to low; simmer until syrup is reduced to 1 1/2 cups, about 15 minutes. Transfer to bowl, cover, and chill. (Can be made 2 days ahead. Keep chilled.)

Ripe passion fruits look dry and very wrinkled. If you can't find them fresh, look for frozen pulp at Latin markets. Or, Monin makes a ready-made passion fruit syrup that you can purchase online if you can't find the fruit you need to make this yourself.

FINALLY! This tart is ready to serve. Remove the chilled tart from the refrigerator. If you used a tart pan with a removable bottom, this is the time to free the tart. Use a small bowl, like a 1 ½ quart mixing bowl, and turn it upside down. Or you can use a large, 28 oz. can of tomatoes.

This becomes the base on which you set the tart pan with its removable bottom. Set the tart on the base and gently tap the top edge. The side ring will slip off and drop to the counter leaving the tart on its base. Carefully transfer the tart to a serving platter for display.

Here's a YouTube video if you want to see how this is done:
https://www.youtube.com/watch?v=UWP4Dei xeXA

Cut the tart into 8 pieces. Place a piece of the tart on a dessert plate and drizzle the top with passion fruit syrup as you serve it.

Coconut Pineapple Sheet Cake
About 40-50 pieces

INGREDIENTS

Cake
2 cups sugar
2 cups all-purpose flour
2eggs
1 (20 ounce) can crushed pineapple with juice
[reserve ¼ cup for frosting]
1 teaspoon baking soda
1 Tahitian vanilla bean, split lengthwise and
seeds scooped out or 1 teaspoon vanilla extract
¼ teaspoon salt

Icing
5 cups powdered sugar
8 ounces softened cream cheese
½ cup chopped macadamia nuts
¼ cup butter, room temperature
1 teaspoon vanilla bean or vanilla extract
Dash of salt [1/4 teaspoon]
¼ cup crushed pineapple
½ cup, shredded, sweetened coconut, toasted

PREPARATION

Cake
Preheat oven to 350 degrees and grease a 13" x
18" or 12" x 18" [half] sheet pan.

Cream butter and sugar, add eggs, pineapple
and vanilla and stir. In a separate bowl, mix

flour, baking soda, and salt, and then combine with wet ingredients. Stir until thoroughly mixed and then pour into prepared pan. Bake for 20-25 minutes. Remove from oven and let it cool.

Icing
Toast the coconut—in the microwave! Spread the ½ cup coconut onto a flat microwave safe plate. Cook using 30 second bursts until it's a golden brown—about 5 minutes if you're coconut is at room temperature when you start. A little longer if it's starts out cold from being stored in the fridge.

Mix all ingredients except coconut to make the icing. Spread evenly over the cooled cake. Sprinkle the toasted coconut on top of the iced cake.

Georgie's Tips

Coconut, pineapple, Tahitian vanilla— wonderful Polynesian, tropical flavors all end up in this cake. If you enjoy that flavor of toasted coconut, make it up ahead of time and store it in the refrigerator. It's great sprinkled on top of pancakes or French toast or as a garnish with a curry dish or even in soup. It'll make an everyday bowl of tomato soup special.

What are the dimensions of a half-sheet cake? Wow! Who knew how much this can vary. Ask your bakery if you order a cake ready-made because sizes are all over the place. The difference in dimensions is tied to do with the fact that the term "sheet cake" more often refers to a flat, single layer style of cake rather than to the pan in which it is baked.

The full-size sheet pans we use in commercial kitchens are 18 inches wide x 26 inches long [too large for most home ovens, btw!]. So, the dimensions here 18 x 13 is based on a sheet pan in half that size. You might find 12 x 18-inch sheet pans are more widely available in stores.

The baking pans most of us have in our homes already are 9 x 13 so quarter-sheet pan sized. They're usually deeper though—more like 3 inches compared to 1 or 2-inch depth in commercial sheet pans. You can use this recipe in a smaller quarter sheet pan, but you will need to cook it longer—30-40 minutes. AND you'll have fewer 2-inch servings [18].

What you get using a half-sheet pan is a thin cake that you can cut into various sizes. You'll get 54 2 x 2-inch [1-inch high] squares that's plenty to go around if you're doing a luau with lots of friends. Make the squares bigger and feed fewer people. Or cook two half-sheets and stack them with filling before icing them!

If you're planning a dessert bar, the smaller slices will make it possible for your guests to try your other treats.

ABOUT THE AUTHOR

Anna Celeste Burke is an award-winning and bestselling author who enjoys *snooping into life's mysteries with fun, fiction, & food—California style!* Her books include the Jessica Huntington Desert Cities Mystery series set in the Coachella Valley near Palm Springs, the Corsario Cove Cozy Mystery series set on California's Central Coast, and The Georgie Shaw Cozy Mystery series set in Orange County, California—*the OC*. Find out more and stay in the loop by joining her at http://www.desertcitiesmystery.com.

CPSIA information can be obtained
at www.ICGtesting.com
Printed in the USA
BVHW041937070521
606800BV00021B/305